The Makeover of

James Orville
Wickenbee

The Makeover of
James Orville Wickenbee

A novel

Anya Bateman

DESERET
BOOK

Salt Lake City, Utah

This is a work of fiction. Characters described in this book are the products of the author's imagination or are represented fictitiously.

© 2006 Anya Bateman

Visit us at deseretbook.com

Library of Congress Publishing Data (on file)

ISBN-10 1-59038-707-4
ISBN-13 978-1-59038-707-8

Printed in the United States of America
Sheridan Books, Chelsea, MI

10   9   8   7   6   5   4   3   2   1

To my father, Jan Copier,
who lived a short but valiant life

Chapter One

If someone had told me a few years ago that I would be sitting here at the Cleveland Hopkins International Airport pressing my knuckles together in anticipation of seeing James Orville Wickenbee again, I would have given that someone what my twin brother, Alex, always called "The Look." He snapped my picture once when I was wearing that expression and hung it on our refrigerator door. "This is so you can see what real attitude looks like," he said.

Well, I'm not wearing "The Look" right now. I'm one humble cookie, sitting far enough away from James's parents, Mary Jane and Rudolf, his brother Felix, and a few others who have also arrived early that so far nobody has noticed me. I don't want to talk to anyone right now. I'm not ready. I need more time to review, to figure things out, to get myself pulled together.

It's doubtful Alex and I would have gotten to know James at all if our Aunt Ruthie hadn't married his older brother Phil. James wasn't our *type*. Alex would chastise me for saying that. Even back then, there were no *types* according to my brother.

"You'll meet Phillip's younger brother, James, at the wedding luncheon," my mother informed us a few days before the wedding. She spoke quietly with a hint of warning; it was the same tone she used when we were little and on our way to visit ritzy Great-Aunt Beatrice's white-carpeted condo. "Ruthie says he's your age," she continued, "and that he goes to Fairport High, too." Her voice held a little too much lilt in it. "The family moved here from Idaho last summer and Ruthie's excited to have you get to know each other."

"How nice," I said. "Idaho." I widened my eyes at Alex, who had no trouble reading my sarcasm. It was my opinion that anything west of Illinois was dirt farm and those who lived there unworthy of a second glance. Alex knew this opinion. He knew all my opinions.

"Give the guy a chance, Jana," my brother said after our mother had moved to the dining area. "You don't even know him."

"Give who a chance—Ruthie's soon-to-be fourth marital disaster, or this younger brother who probably looks and acts exactly like him?"

"Both!"

I readjusted myself in the leather recliner and pushed the book I was reading for A.P. English, *Crime and Punishment*, against the armrest. I was sure that Ruthie, our mother's artistic, flamboyant younger sister and my favorite relative, was about to throw herself away on someone so far beneath her that under normal circumstances, he would have had to take a number just for the privilege of standing at the back of the line to meet her. I was also sure I knew why our aunt was about to make what I considered a colossal mistake.

"I guess we can't blame Ruthie for picking someone who's about as opposite of Flashy Floyd as you can get," I said to Alex, misery thickening my voice.

He grunted his agreement and nodded slowly.

"Flashy Floyd" was our nickname for Ruthie's previous husband, her third. "But honestly," I whined. "This guy—"

"Phillip is a practicing Mormon, so he doesn't drink even a little," our mother, who can hear through cement, assured us from the dining room where she was sifting through the drawer of the rosewood cabinet. She was alluding to the fact that Ruthie's first two husbands *did* drink—like fish. "And he isn't at all the type to run around."

"Well, thank the stars for that," I said as Mom came back into the study, smoothing some lavender luncheon napkins against her palm. I restrained myself from adding that I didn't feel *Phillip Wickenbee* was someone anyone would want to be caught dead running around *with*. Flashy Floyd, on the other hand, had had little trouble finding himself playmates while he was married to our aunt, and had wined and dined them on Ruthie's funds. In other words, the snake had taken our sweet, naïve auntie to the cleaners. That's why after three marital strikes against her, I was highly concerned that Ruthie not make yet another equally bad blunder on the opposite end of the spectrum; it's also why I asked my mother to repeat the first part of what she'd just said.

"Phillip is Mormon—a member of what he calls The Church of Jesus Christ of Latter-day Saints." Mom lowered her voice and looked around as though she thought the CIA or worse, the ladies from her charity league, might be listening.

My voice was not at all lowered. "A Mormon? My stars! This is so much worse than I thought! Aren't Mormons so strict they can't even drink coffee or tea?"

"Mormons are good family people," my mother let me know.

I huffed out my scorn. "Yes, I guess that does explain the fifteen-year age gap between Phillip and this younger brother. There are probably, what, a dozen siblings in between?"

"I believe Phillip said there are eight children in the family," Mom said, searching through the desk drawer for, I assumed, more napkins for her annual early November Ladies' Afternoon Tea. "Phillip is the oldest and this James, who is your age, is the youngest. Two are missionaries for their church and the rest are married and have families, and live here or in Utah or Idaho." She looked up. "No, now wait, I think Phillip said one brother and his family live in Fresno, California." She glanced around her once again and whispered, "He's a bishop there. In the Mormon faith that's like a pastor."

I turned to my brother who was playing Golf-Pro on the computer. "Did you hear that?" I moaned. "This Phillip's a Mormon from a *ten*-Mormon family, Alex! What's Ruthie thinking? They'll soon be recruiting her to join their church, of course, because that's what they do. This is so much worse than I thought. I've got to talk to her again!" Not that I thought it would do any good. My last expression of concern had not caused the slightest ripple in my aunt's resolve.

"Hey, I don't care if this Phillip's a Shaker or a Quaker or drives around in a buggy or has a fear of toasters as long as he's good to her," Alex replied without taking his eyes from his game. "Ruthie deserves to be happy."

Alex was referring to the Amish who reside in Middlefield and several other towns just outside of Cleveland. Or is it the Mennonites who don't use toasters? There's even a religious group that doesn't believe in buttons. Buttons or coffee, I saw little difference. I lumped what I considered the ridiculously strict churches together in one big wad.

"There's a lot more to life than being happy!" I snapped.

Alex turned to look at me, his eyebrows knitted together. Mom exited the room again, *her* eyebrows raised and shaking her head.

Chapter Two

S ure enough, that following Thursday at the wedding luncheon, Alex and I found our place cards on what Mom had
designated as "the young adult table" right next to the card
labeled *James Orville Wickenbee.*

"Wonderful," I whispered, flipping open my napkin.

As things turned out, I was *underneath* the young adult table by
the time James arrived. Aunt Nadine, my mother's other younger
sister, had asked Alex and me to keep an eye on our two-and-a-
half-year-old cousin Reginald while she checked on the catering
and made sure everything was running smoothly. Apparently
Reggie's nanny had bailed out at the last minute. I couldn't blame
the woman for not wanting to work overtime. You had to keep
much more than just "an eye" on Reggie.

Ironically, I'd been so fearful the Wickenbees would turn the
wedding luncheon into a mommy-and-me affair that I'd talked
Aunt Ruthie into stressing that small children were to be left with

sitters. Now here *I* was struggling to pull the only toddler here—and from *our* side of the family—away from the table leg to which he'd attached himself. It was embarrassing. Alex tapped me on my back and said pleasantly, "Jana, come up a second and meet James."

"Oh . . . yes . . . hello." I emerged for three, possibly four seconds—just long enough to take James's extended hand, nod, and manage a smile. Then I actually felt fortunate I had an excuse to go back underneath the table. There I widened my eyes and tucked in my lips. Just exactly as I had predicted, James, though taller and thinner than Phillip, was a fifteen-year-younger replica. He was even wearing the same style of strange, outdated glasses. All the Wickenbee brothers, at least those I'd met thus far, looked remarkably alike. But James and Phillip? These two were stamped out. Oh, how I wanted to whisper to Alex that somebody up there had a wry sense of humor.

Unfortunately, I had other, more immediate challenges, namely dealing with Reggie. I had no sooner unfastened him from the table leg than he broke loose from my grasp and headed straight for the indoor water fountain, intent, I suspected, on diving in. By the time I'd tackled him and carried him back to our table, Alex and James were deep in conversation. Alex can talk to anybody about anything, but terms such as "nuclear fusion" indicated that this was not your typical get-acquainted small talk.

I didn't care if they were coming up with a cure for cancer. With raised eyebrows and with Reginald in a straddle-hold under my arm, I waited to get Alex's attention to let him know that I needed a break from tending our not-so-cute-at-the-moment baby cousin, and I needed one *now*. I was about to simply dump the little guy in Alex's lap when James stopped mid-sentence and peered at me. "You need some help," he stated flatly.

"Excuse me?"

"I said it looks like you could use some help with that little tyke."

"You're telling me," I said. Reggie had somehow managed to reach a butter knife and was in the process of buttering my arm. The "little tyke" was getting entirely too close to the three-quarter-length sleeve of the raw silk afternoon dress I'd been lucky enough to find for half price at Talbot's. I grabbed Alex's napkin. "Do you happen to have a small straitjacket with you, James?"

"Just a minute." James immediately left the table.

I looked at Alex in puzzlement as I attempted to turn Reggie right side up. "He's getting one? I thought I was kidding."

But a few seconds later James returned with a booster chair. In several more seconds he had a napkin tucked around Reggie's neck and was patiently explaining to him that the shrimp he was feeding him were actually little sea creatures that had once lived in the ocean.

"Why day come wedding?" Reggie asked.

I snorted and looked over at Alex who laughed aloud. Reggie was quickly regaining adorability status. Although it was hard to tell behind his glasses, even James seemed amused.

"I appreciate this, James," I admitted as I neatly spooned cocktail sauce onto a small white plate and scanned the shrimp bowl for the largest and healthiest of the little "sea creatures."

"No problem at all. I have fourteen nieces and nephews so I'm used to kids." James pushed back his glasses, which were sliding down his nose.

"Well, hopefully you've never had to tend them all at once," I responded flippantly.

When he smiled, I noted that at least his teeth weren't bad. The rest of him—oh dear. I wasn't sure where a person could find a suit that horrible even if he were looking for one. *How*, I wondered, *can anyone be so clueless?* Still, I really couldn't have a completely negative opinion about someone who had just given me an opportunity to enjoy what looked like a savory meal. The house salad had arrived and the cordon bleu was in the process of being served. Yes, it was decent of James to see my plight and jump in to help.

Inspired by James's good example, Alex was also soon keeping Reggie interested in proper behavior—or at least sidetracking him from really poor behavior. By taking turns, the task of tending little Reginald eased considerably, and we could each enjoy, for small segments of time anyway, some truly fine dining.

Still, I did not smile back at Alex when he raised his eyebrows at me with a "See, this guy isn't half bad" message. It would take more than a little baby-sitting talent to impress me, and my brother needed to understand that.

"Yes, I admit James is a nice enough person, and he even has surprisingly good table manners," I clarified to Alex later that night as I brushed out my hair in the bathroom. "And I admit even Ruthie's Phil showed a little more personality today. But I still say this is a classic rebound situation. By going to the opposite end of the spectrum, Aunt Ruthie has overcorrected like you do in a car just before you crash on the other side of the median. Honestly,

Alex, did you really look at those two brothers? Did you take a good look at the man Ruthie will be sitting across the dining table from for the rest of her life?" I handed Alex the whitening toothpaste that I'd recommended he start using.

"What's wrong with the way he looks?" Alex ignored the hint and squeezed a blob of generic toothpaste onto his toothbrush.

It was such a guy reply. I soaked a white monogrammed washcloth in the warm water and held it against my cheek. "Ruthie didn't need to jump into this. She could have eventually married someone who at least doesn't dress like a boor. And then just maybe he would have had a younger brother to match instead of this James Orville person. I'm not talking flashy," I added quickly, raising one hand so that Alex wouldn't bring up Aunt Ruthie's previous marital catastrophes. "There are sober, ethically intact, morally sound, *nice* people out there who are relatively attractive and know how to dress as well."

I didn't add that my brother himself was a perfect example of the kind of person I was talking about. Granted, Alex could get a touch lazy once in a while when it came to his grooming habits and his manners in general, for that matter—he wasn't what you'd call fastidious, by any means—but for the most part he had a stylishness that enhanced his sporty good looks. There was a good reason why girls followed my fair-haired brother around the school halls. "There are relatively nice men out there who at least have some degree of class," I continued.

"I guess we must have a different definition of *class*," said Alex, "because after talking to James, I'm impressed. Maybe he doesn't have some of the *finishing touches* you'd like, but he's a good, decent, and really interesting guy."

I started to point out to Alex that the term "finishing touches" was an understatement the size of Baltimore, but Alex didn't give me a chance.

"And I haven't really talked that much to Phil, but if he's as smart as his little brother . . ." Alex looked at my reflection in the mirror. "In the few minutes I talked to James, I got the impression this dude is brighter than you and me put together."

"Really," I scoffed. Alex knew that my ACT score was already high enough to get me into some of the top colleges. I had a 3.98 GPA, which would have been a 4.0 if Mr. Wrigley, last year's algebra teacher, hadn't been so hard-nosed about giving As. Nevertheless, in my less than humble opinion, I felt it would be extremely difficult to be smarter than I was—even solo. And though he rarely made much effort to prove it, Alex was far from being a dunce himself. Finding someone smarter than both of us put together would, I felt, have been about as likely as finding an emerald in a walnut.

But there are different ways of being smart. I'd learned the hard way that IQ has little to do with getting ahead in the world.

"So how smart can you be and not notice that your glasses look like circus clown props?" I asked aloud. The way James dressed was reason enough, as far as I was concerned, for my brother to steer clear of him at school. I had plans for Alex, and I didn't want this James Orville Wickenbee entering the picture and ruining things.

"Alex, please tell me you'll just acknowledge him, you know, nod and be polite if you see him in the halls, of course, but then leave it at that." I was almost pleading. "I just don't want people to get the wrong impression of who you—well, who *we* are." Even as I said the words I knew how they would sound to Alex, but I said them anyway because they needed to be said.

"You'd avoid someone because of his glasses?" Alex responded with predictable disgust.

I moved the washcloth to my other cheek. "Yes, if that person peers at you over them like some kind of barn owl. And no, that's not the only reason. Heavenly stars, Alex, he's a Mormon! Sure, I know what you're thinking. You're thinking why should I even care what kind of ugly glasses James wears or whether or not he worships golden angels. But you know why I care."

"Oh, please, not again," Alex moaned. "I really don't want to hear this again."

"But Alex, you could soooooo easily—"

Alex backed out of the bathroom. "Don't say it. I mean it. I'm warning you, I have heard this so many times that I might go eat Sheetrock if I have to hear it again."

It was true I'd shared with Alex numerous times my belief that if he jumped through the right hoops, he could become the next student body president of Fairport High. My sharp tongue hadn't endeared me to many, but Alex was, and I suspected always would be, a natural when it came to winning friends and influencing people.

When my brother walked into a room, it came to life. There was an unspoken, *Okay, Alex is here; the party can begin.* My brother was born with the talent to get people laughing, talking, joking, and even singing. My role in his life, as I saw it, was to help him use this talent to get somewhere, to *be* somebody. It would start at Fairport, and then . . . who knew? With a little help from me, I was certain that nothing would stop Alex from reaching dizzying heights. "You could become a congressman someday if you played your cards right," I'd let him know quite a few times.

I wasn't alone in my opinion. Our adorable and wonderful Uncle Bartholomew, Mom's older brother, had once indicated that he, too, thought Alex had the right stuff. After serving on several boards and in an appointed government position, Uncle Bartho had been urged by many to enter politics himself. He had been seriously considering it, and I believe would have done so had his life not been cut short. "Your brother," he'd told me once, "has that rare combination of charisma *and* intelligence. He's a natural leader."

I agreed. Even rarer was Alex's combination of good looks and good character.

I was certain that Uncle Bartho had not really been joking when he'd teased Alex about becoming president of the United States someday. There was nothing funny about it. With the right connections, Alex could climb sky-high in government. But in politics, image is important and in high school, where I planned to launch Alex's political career, image is *everything*.

"It's who you know and who you're seen with," I'd told him. What I perceived as Alex's naïveté when it came to his choice of friends was just about the only thing I could think of that would stop him from landing the school's top student position. I was fearful that his very goodness and friendliness toward *everyone* would backfire. And that's why I was nervous about this cama-raderie that had developed so quickly between him and James.

As I patted my face dry on a white, satin-edged, mono-grammed hand towel, I repeated, "Just be careful who you're seen with. That's all I'm asking."

Alex leaned against the bathroom door. His eyes met mine. "You know what? You're hopeless." He shook his head and turned down the hall to his bedroom.

"Oh, so now I'm hopeless," I repeated as I looked in the mir-ror, bobbling my head. When my mouth began to droop down-ward ever so slightly and my eyes started to lose a little glow, I quickly lifted my chin, lowered my lids, and hung up the towel. Still my stomach hurt a little as I crawled into bed. The skeletons in my closet were doing their little rain dance again.

Chapter Three

I n spite of my pleas, Alex made it clear he didn't care about image. He visited with James, laughed with James, and hung out with James Orville Wickenbee right out in the open, right in the front hall of Fairport.

"Is James suddenly your best friend or something?" I asked Alex the night after he'd invited James to eat with us at our lunch table. I had carefully handpicked certain people to join us there, and it had been far from easy to convince some of them to come to our table. It wasn't as if I enjoyed brownnosing. I was doing it for him.

"No, I wouldn't say James is my best friend—not yet, anyway," said Alex, sliding on a Joe's Tires cap he'd picked up from who knew where.

"Yet?" I repeated, ripping off the cap. "Do you want to know what Dolly Devonshire said?" I flipped him his Cleveland Indians ball cap, which was not much of a step up, but at least not quite as blue-collar.

"Not really," Alex said, adjusting the cap carefully on his head as he perused the pantry for an on-the-road meal.

I told him anyway. "Dolly said, 'What poor little puppy has Alex brought home to our table now?'"

"Mm-hm," mumbled Alex as he pulled out a can of pears and shifted it from hand to hand. "That's nice."

"That's nice? I think it's a pretty insightful comment for Dolly Devonshire." Around school, Dolly was known more for her physical attributes than her insight or intellect. "I'd say she has you tabbed!"

For as long as I could remember, Alex had brought home strays: dogs mostly, a few scraggly cats, one duck, a tortoise, and even an iguana that escaped out a basement window and ended up surprising our snooty Chicago neighbor Mrs. Aldrose in the shower the next day.

"You know what? I really don't care what Dolly Devonshire has to say." Alex pulled out a bag of tortilla chips. "Or what your other supposed friends think."

"Well, maybe you should care!"

Lyla Fannen was among those I'd finally recruited to join us. She and Dolly and Sonja Paulos had had some trouble deciding which table of popular people they would grace with their presence and (when they weren't driving up to the Lake for lunch at exclusive restaurants) had been table-hopping all through September and October.

But to my amazement, when November rolled around, the

three girls started eating exclusively at our table. I still couldn't believe Lyla had apparently chosen to remain with us because Lyla was *the* person to know at Fairport. Even *I* wasn't sure how she'd risen so quickly to star status. Oh sure, her ultra-expensive fashion sense helped, as did her finely chiseled cheekbones and her amazingly gorgeous fox-red hair. She was, without a doubt, the most beautiful girl at our school. But there are lots of beautiful people who get nowhere in this life. I guessed it was the "I'm somebody" lift of her head that made her a standout. Or was it her "You're nobody" sneer? Whatever it was, I'm appalled to admit now that I actually *respected* where it had gotten her.

Dolly struck me as little more than a loosey-goosey with the clothes to match, but these three were some of the right people who ran around with others who were the right people: Jessica Bjorn, Courtney Martindale, Katrina Utley and her cousin Scott Wilkes—Fairport's answer to Brad Pitt. They were stopping by our table now as was svelte, golden-skinned super-model Shereen Quinn. The jocks and preps at the adjacent tables, among them Carson Parker and Dan Ravino, often called to us from their tables as well. Yes, later, I told myself, we'd concentrate on cultivating real friends. But right now, I let Alex know, we shouldn't be too proud to grovel.

The really amazing part, as far as I was concerned, was that Lyla had not immediately picked up her Louis Vuitton purse, gathered up her friends, and vamoosed the scene the instant James appeared. To my relief, she'd merely lifted an eyebrow and whispered to me, "Interesting glasses." But if James continued to join us for lunch, I was certain Lyla Fannen would not stick to a mere eyebrow lift. People like Lyla didn't associate with people like James.

"Do *not* have James come to our lunch table again," I said to Alex again that night after dinner. "I mean it, Alex. I've done far too much work to have *him* ruin everything." Yes, those were my words.

"And just why are you doing this so-called *work?*" Alex responded with frustration, maybe even hostility in his voice.

"For you, of course."

"Who asked you?"

I didn't answer.

But after Alex had gone downstairs to our newly remodeled recreation room in order to catch the last of the Cavaliers' game on the big screen, I found myself frowning at my thumbnail. Why *did* I feel so compelled to have Alex become president of our school, regardless of the cost?

It was the kind of thing Dr. Griffin would have tried to pull out of me. I'd gone to his office for several weeks of therapy the summer after what Alex and Mom and I still refer to as "that awful period," but which for me had been so much worse than awful that no adjective was strong enough. At first I'd felt fine talking to Dr. Griffin, but then I stopped going because Dr. Griffin kept prodding me to reveal more than I wanted to divulge. *Why should I tell things to someone I'd just barely met that even my twin brother doesn't know?* I remember thinking.

Chapter Four

ꙮ

A flight has apparently just arrived because passengers are swarming into the waiting area of the airport. Airport terminals are very much like high school halls and college corridors in that you see all colors, sizes, classes, and types of people. You see the tall, the short, and the in-between. You see those who have let themselves go, and others who have kept themselves in excellent shape. You see people wearing stylish, well thought-out clothing, and you see those wearing strange, paltry, or far too little clothing. You see people who seem to be with it, and others who don't seem to fit in and look as though they never will. There are the talkative and the stoic, the outgoing and the shy. You can generally spot the troublemakers, but you can pick out the well-behaved and civilized as well. At least you think you can.

At the airport there's a much wider range of ages, of course. Take that man in the corner who looks like he's well into his eighties. He seems to be waiting for the forty-something woman in the tasteless shorts. Hopefully she is his daughter or granddaughter rather than his wife or who knows what. And over there it's family reunion time as an orange-haired woman gives a bearded man in cowboy gear a huge hug, while a younger, nine- or ten-year-old version of the woman yelps with joy.

My mouth twitches into a small smile until I see the thirty-something businesswoman, carrying a sleek briefcase and wearing high-heeled shoes, glancing with disdain at the little family as she clips past them. With obvious annoyance she pushes away the balloons that James's parents have brought to celebrate his return. Yes, there are all kinds of people.

And thanks to James, those I'd tabbed as the "questionable" and "unacceptable" characters of Fairport High were soon flocking around Alex like Merry Men (and Maid Marians) who had found their Robin Hood.

There was Terrance Dokey, who strode down the school halls with his mouth open and his arms held tightly at his sides as if they were strapped there.

With his tousle of Conan O'Brien-style hair, Derrick Farn looked a great deal like a human rooster pecking into the air as he moved from class to class.

Sadie Rice, his cousin, seemed to have a perpetual sinus condition. I hadn't seen much of her face, thanks to limp hair that hung down her cheeks like nearly closed curtains.

Her best, and possibly only friend, Cassie Beudka was not shy—no, not in the least. Cassie shouted out her trademark "Wowsers!" with such vigor that you could hear her halfway across the school. *Wowsers?* What normal person said that? It wasn't as if

Cassie needed to draw attention to herself. She was as large as an apartment building, and when *she* walked down the halls, unwary freshmen were knocked over like bowling pins.

Cassie's brother, Bud, on the other hand, looked like something that had just slid out of a pasta maker. He was extremely tall and extraordinarily underweight.

But it was James himself, however, who remained Alex's favorite sidekick. Or was it the other way around?

"What on earth do you two talk about?" I finally asked. I was very concerned about this strange alliance. In a matter of weeks Alex would need to submit his intent to run for a school office and there wasn't much time left for him to let those I'd recruited to join us for lunch know he was one of *them* and not one of *the others.* It was obvious that James would be the most difficult to rid ourselves of. He was joining us at our lunch table every day now where he ate obscenely huge sandwiches he'd made himself.

"What *don't* we talk about?" Alex grinned. "James and I talk about everything: computers, science, history—ask James anything about history."

"Since when are you interested in history?" I'd already put in my time on the treadmill this morning. Now I was applying fingernail polish and watching Alex work out.

"I'm interested in anything that's interesting. For instance, James told me that back in about 400 A.D. there was a religious dude who, get this, lived on top of a pole for *thirty-seven* years."

"Why?"

"Something about self-denial and keeping himself away from the world and its temptations."

That was, I had to admit, a pretty interesting tidbit—one that confirmed that people have done and still do some very strange and even harmful things in the name of religion. But an interesting story now and again didn't seem like enough reason for my brother to jeopardize his future.

"Why don't you just register for an extra night class to learn these things? That way you'd get a head start on your college credit. I could check into it and see if you're eligible."

"Even sports history," Alex said, ignoring my suggestion. "James really knows his stats. Did you know that Reggie Jackson struck out 2,597 times? That's six hundred more times than the guy with the next highest number of strikeouts. But the point is, he also hit 563 home runs." Alex paused, picked up one of his twenty-pound weights, and pulled it toward him four or five times. He stopped abruptly. "Oh, and we play chess."

I lifted my head and looked at my brother with suspicion. He had presented this last fact far too casually. I didn't care an eyelash about how many outs or hits Reggie Jackson had to his credit, but Alex was fully aware of how strongly I felt about the game of chess.

Uncle Bartholomew had introduced Alex and me to the game as soon as we were old enough to sit at the board. Alex wasn't a bad player, but I had taken to chess like a seagull to Lake Erie. I was, as a matter of fact, obsessed with the game and determined to win the Teen to Young Adult Ohio State Chess Championship that spring. I'd studied chess-strategy books all that summer before, but I had one significant problem.

Since I was trying to keep a low profile and not really advertise what I was doing until I had actually won, I belonged to no chess groups and therefore really didn't have anyone who could properly challenge me in practice matches. My Uncle Charles, though a somewhat better player than Alex, was out of town most of the time. Mom was capable of playing a fairly decent game of chess, but didn't have the patience or interest to play her best and was far too busy with her causes. Besides I never knew if she was really trying or just happy to let me win. I'd even attempted to teach Adriana, my friend since the beginning of our sophomore year, how to play and she had definite potential, but she was much more interested in keeping current on social affairs at school than improving her chess skills.

"Is he any good?" I asked, reapplying fingernail polish to my right pinky where it had smeared.

"Good?" Alex half laughed. "Oh, yeah."

"Really?"

Alex shifted the weight to his other hand. "You can come watch us play if you want to."

I blew on my nail.

"I mean it. You ought to come. It's fun to see genius in action. The guy's amazing."

"But how would *you* know, really?"

Alex took the insult in stride. "Let's just say he creams me much worse than you ever have. I think he's better than you are."

I pushed my mouth forward. Alex was doing his best to get to me, and I didn't want to admit it, but he was succeeding. "So if he's that good is he planning on entering any chess tournaments?"

"I don't think he does those kinds of competitions. At least he didn't sound interested when I told him about them. He's pretty heavily into physics and chemistry experiments and computers. That and his church stuff. You only have so much time."

"Well, maybe I *will* come see for myself . . ." Alex gets this certain kind of annoyingly satisfied look on his face when he thinks he's scored points or is winning in a contest between us. "And maybe I won't," I finished, blowing on my nail again. I didn't want Alex thinking I was some kind of pushover.

"Hey, ask me if I care. It's totally up to you." Alex was still lifting the weight toward the ceiling. I kept blowing on my nail even though it had to be dry by this time. The words "It's up to you" were the best words anyone could say to me. Mom had finally caught on and now she said those words entirely too much. Just last month, she'd reminded me that it was "up to me" whether or not to join the Cleveland Young Women's Cultural Club. "But keep in mind," she'd added, "that you would meet girls from some of the best families in the Cleveland Heights area. Still, you're the one who knows what you want."

And now Alex was using the same psychology. Or was he? I wasn't sure. Maybe he really meant the words. Maybe he really didn't care. I decided that regardless of whether my brother was *trying* to get me to go with him to James's, it didn't matter—if I decided to go, it would be because *I* wanted to go.

Chapter Five

ᴑᴑᴑ

E ven though the term "living room" suggests a room in which you actually "live," the rooms I was familiar with acted more as showcases. Ours contains two cream-white couches we rarely sat on; some eighteenth-century chairs we were not to even think about touching; a variety of original sculptures and paintings; several Henredon tables with lamps; and an outrageously expensive Aubusson rug Great-Aunt Beatrice left us when she died.

In contrast, the Wickenbees really did seem to *live* in their living room. A huge old desk with a globe in one corner was stacked with mail, papers, pamphlets, books, magazines, and newspapers. The bookcase above it, which extended across the entire wall, was spilling over its shelves. There were some additional boxes filled with books that apparently hadn't been unloaded since the family's move from Idaho. I walked over and thumbed through a few titles, impressed by the collection.

Next I studied some artwork on the bulletin board next to the
alcove that led into the kitchen. One drawing entitled "Grandma"
depicted a rather out-of-proportion human being with arms that
came to her ankles. It didn't actually look that much different than
some pieces I'd seen in the San Francisco Museum of Modern Art.
The rest of the board was filled with wedding announcements,
photographs, and quotes. Then there was a picture of a manger
with the question: "Are you part of the *inn* crowd or one of the
stable few?"

A large, square coffee table supporting a stack of magazines, a
Boston fern, and an enormous dictionary stood in the middle of
the room equidistant from two oversized corduroy chairs and a big
blue couch with a sinkhole in it.

I moseyed over to a card table which was set up in the corner
and stood with my arms folded, watching Alex and James play on
the well-worn chessboard. When it comes to chess, of course, it's
more like watching people *not* play. For long periods of time
there's not a great deal happening. Still, it wasn't at all hard to tell
what had gone on before. Seven of Alex's pieces, including a rook,
a knight, and a bishop, had been removed from the board. James,
on the other hand, had only lost three pawns. It was obvious that
my brother was losing badly. James graciously tried to pretend
otherwise.

"Alex has been playing a pretty good game," he said.

"Right, uh-huh." Alex laughed. "The truth is James is killing
me again. But hey, I'm learning a lot."

"You still have a chance," I snapped, studying the board carefully. If he concentrated, Alex could at least save himself from

complete annihilation. If he moved his rook to the left—why wasn't he paying more attention? It bothered me that my brother was taking a potential loss so lightly.

James remained kind. "Are you sure you want to move there?" he asked when Alex slid the rook forward.

"Yes, are you sure?" I repeated. I turned to James. "He's not sure!" My fingers were aching to pick up that rook and move it for my brother, but I restrained myself.

Alex chuckled good-naturedly. "Oh, boy, what am I missing now?" He scooted his chair closer and studied the board carefully. "Oh-ho, dude, I think I see what you mean."

I looked back at James, confused and a little awed. Had he kept his mouth shut, he could have checkmated Alex's king in two more moves. Why wasn't James more interested in winning the game? Several more times during the following half hour, James asked Alex, "Are you sure you don't want to rethink that?"

Again and again, Alex would study the situation, grin, and once more pursue a new route. At first I felt relief for Alex and gratitude toward James, but then gradually I began to find James's charity patronizing. Why didn't he just go for the jugular? Why didn't he just finish Alex off? That's what I would have done. It was a game, wasn't it—a competition?

An hour later, James finally put Alex out of his misery. Actually, maybe I should say that he put *me* out of my misery. That he'd lost and lost badly seemed to be bothering me more than my brother.

"Good game," Alex said. "I learned a lot."

"I'll play you next time, James," I heard myself say.

"You want to be cremated too, huh?" Alex joked.

"We'll see," I said.

The following Saturday, James Orville Wickenbee and I began playing our first of what would ultimately be many chess matches. Once again, James was irritatingly gracious. Once again, he kept trying to aid and assist, only this time, he was trying to help *me*.

"Are you sure you want to move there?" he asked when I scooted a knight forward and to the left.

"Excuse me," I said, lifting my eyebrows at him. "Let me make something very clear. I don't require any help. Even if I did need your help, I wouldn't want it. Just play the best game you can and I will as well and good luck to you."

"Oh . . . okay, sorry." The next word to come out of James's mouth was "Checkmate."

I hadn't seen it coming, and I stared at the board in complete astonishment. I could not for the life of me figure out how what had just happened could have happened. "Okay, tell me how you did that," I finally said.

James kindly did an instant replay.

"Hmmmm . . . okay . . . Oh, I see." Just as Alex had predicted, I'd been humiliated royally, but oddly, I wasn't that upset about it. In fact, when James got up to get us some glasses of ice water, I rubbed my hands together. James was truly a brilliant chess player. I'd never seen anyone that good. Better yet, if Alex was correct, the guy apparently wasn't interested in entering any of the chess competitions. That meant I could learn from James—allow him to be my mentor—and then use everything he taught me in my competitions. By being patient now, taking some losses during the next month or two, I'd reap bigger rewards later. Yes, maybe James would be winning every game for a while, but I'd be the big winner in the end.

In December I organized my time carefully so that I could continue having afternoon practice matches with James every Saturday. Luckily I'd done most of my Christmas shopping far ahead of time. On Saturdays I woke up early to finish papers and homework and chores, and headed to James's in the afternoon. And when the Christmas break hit, I convinced my brother to stop by James's several times with me so I could get a really good workout.

I was so impressed with what I was learning that I even declined Mom's invitation to go to the mayor's annual Christmas open house for city volunteers at the mansion. Instead I became a human sponge as James openly shared with me his techniques. I considered this highly generous of him and okay, *classy.*

Once in a while I would notice and appreciate the kind of simple homespun Christmas the Wickenbees celebrated. I'd actually forgotten what a real tree smelled like. It was nice. The Wickenbees' homemade paper chains and potluck decorations were quite a contrast to the elegant European silk and crystal decorations that Mom and I had hung on our tree, each one equally spaced apart.

The caramel popcorn Mary Jane kept bringing out was tempting, but mostly I stuck with the fruit that was also in ample supply. I did indulge in a tiny bit of fudge, but knew then as I still know now, that the holiday season can play havoc on your weight if you're not careful.

In keeping with the Christmas spirit, James loaned me some

of his chess books, even the one that was translated from Russian and which he claimed was the *bible* of chess.

"You realize I'm going to use these strategies against you now," I said, in an unChristmaslike manner.

"I hope you do."

"And you don't care if I defeat you one of these days?"

"It's just a game."

"Yes, but that's all life is anyway, isn't it—a game?"

James smiled. "Shakespeare says something like that in *Macbeth*—that life isn't much more than 'a poor player that struts and frets his hour upon the stage—'"

"'A tale told by an idiot, full of sound and fury, signifying nothing,'" I quoted with him. We smiled at each other with mutual respect.

"So do you believe that?" James asked. "I don't, but it's a good quote."

"What *do* you believe?" I almost asked, but I stopped myself. I'd heard about Mormons and how they operated. There was no way I wanted to listen to a lengthy religious presentation. His last comment, I was sure, had been the bait at the end of a fishing line. Well, I wasn't biting. As a matter of fact, I think I'd been subconsciously waiting for this to happen—much like you wait for the sales pitch when you know someone is selling cosmetics. Still, I had to admit that even a discourse on Mormonism probably wouldn't be boring if presented by James O.

It had taken me several weeks to figure out what Alex had discovered in just a few minutes: James was extremely interesting to be around. He seemed to know something about everything and, like me, read voraciously. I became so fascinated with the things that he told me that there were a couple of days toward the end of the break that I didn't even notice what he was wearing or how he looked.

The last Saturday of the break, I finally admitted to myself that James was not only a stimulating conversationalist, but one of those rare and almost extinct beings—a good listener. I had no choice but to acknowledge that I was beginning to highly respect James Orville Wickenbee. It did not, however, mean I planned to allow him to act as a roadblock to my brother's high school successes in student government! I wasn't about to let anything or anyone derail me in *that* endeavor.

"I think I can understand why you like to spend time with James after school," I finally admitted to Alex the second Saturday into the new semester after we'd come back from playing chess and visiting at the Wickenbees' house. "But you still need to do your best to stay away from him *at* school. *I've* already established an appropriate relationship with him. James knows that visiting with me in the halls is off-limits so he barely speaks to me there. But he's still happy to play chess with me on Saturdays. I really don't think he'd mind if you avoided him whenever there are people around who might notice. I honestly think he'd understand, Alex. I mean, we can handle James individually—but his friends, Alex? My stars, there's a whole tribe of them and they won't leave you and James alone! You're going to have to do something!" My brother stared at me as if I were mold on a roast beef sandwich.

Later that night, however, he caught up with me in the kitchen.

"Look, I know why you're doing what you're doing," he said, his voice compassionate and lower than usual. "It's not hard to figure out. I know why you want me to be president of Fairport so badly."

"Oh, are you going to analyze me again?"

"Yes. It's called compensation. You're trying to climb your way out of our past, and you think you can use me as some kind of a ladder or hoist."

"Well, thank you, Dr. Griffin." My first instinct—call it my debate training—was to counter him. "First of all, I'd hardly call it our *past*. We had a fairly decent *past* with the exception of that awful period. We were only in the situation you're referring to for four or five months—an extremely small percentage of our lives."

I suddenly had a bad taste in my mouth. Who was I trying to fool? Even a few minutes of trauma could alter a life, and we'd had much more than a few minutes of trauma during that awful period we were all doing our best to forget. Still, I didn't need Alex's pity.

"Secondly, I don't see *you* as the hoist," I said, quickly changing my approach. "If I'm not mistaken, I'm the one pulling you up where you belong. Think about it, Alex. You have a chance to lead a school." Then, appealing to his altruistic nature, I added, "You could make a genuine difference."

"As long as I step on a friend or two to get there? No thanks." It was obvious that my brother still wasn't planning to cooperate, and it frustrated me when he grabbed his coat, walked out into the cold night, and slammed the back door, refusing to talk about it anymore.

I sat at the table and stared at the door with my chin on the heel of my hand, blinking profusely. The truth was I wasn't happy myself about some of my methods. The more time I spent with James Orville Wickenbee, the more I admired, respected, and cared about him. In fact, it was more than that. I think that was the moment I finally and completely admitted to myself that I genuinely and sincerely *liked* this deep-thinking interesting guy with his dry sense of humor and his quirky "Who cares?" appearance.

Chapter Six

The more I associated with those I secretly called "the hollow people" of Fairport, the more I looked forward to Saturdays when I could relax in the Wickenbees' cluttered, but fascinating living room. The two to three hours I spent there felt like an oasis in my otherwise arid life. Social climbing for Alex's sake was really beginning to take its toll on me. Pretending I was one of the shallow lovelies of the school took a supreme effort on my part. In James's living room, on the other hand, I could relax and be completely who I really was. Alex, James, and I talked honestly about books, music, philosophy, politics, and life. Sometimes Alex would bring an old classic movie from his vast collection and watch it while James and I played our game.

On the Saturdays when Alex had soccer practice, just James and I would play chess, talk, and hang out with his family. Absurd as it sounds now, I went to great lengths to avoid being seen going into James's house by anyone from school, however. I not only parked around the corner, but I would pull my hat down or wear sunglasses or sneak from bush to tree like I was a spy or a common thief.

I considered it fortunate that most of the elite lived nearer to Lake Erie, but Brittany Cunningham, the editor of our school paper and one of Lyla's most devout followers, lived only two blocks away. I was completely paranoid that she'd catch Alex or me going into James's house and snap our picture. Brittany was notorious for catching Fairport students in embarrassing situations. That fall she'd sneaked to the rear of Cassie Beudka and snapped her picture just as Cassie bent over to bob for apples at the Halloween party. It was something Cassie had mentioned several times and laughed about a little too often.

Every so often Phil and Ruthie stopped by the Wickenbees' with Chinese, pizza, chicken, or even sushi and Alex and I would stay and eat. Though the Wickenbees invited Alex and me to eat with them at other times as well, we always declined in spite of the fact that the simple meals began to look very appealing after a while. Finally the stews, casseroles, Crock-Pot dishes, and even leftovers, though far from gourmet, began to look so good to me that I asked James if his mother would like a part-time job, explaining that our mother had been trying for months to get some decent help in the kitchen.

"My mother already has a part-time job," James said. "She's a freelance chemist for Packer-Done." It turned out Mary Jane had a Ph.D. He took me down to the family's basement lab one day and filled me in on the things his mother had been cooking up outside her kitchen. Then he happily showed me some of his own experiments.

Although it was obvious Mary Jane didn't subscribe to *House Beautiful,* she was nevertheless no different than any other woman in that she was concerned about her home's appearance. "I cleared out so much when we moved that I thought we'd be clutter-free in this new larger house. But now it's almost as if it's all back again," she complained. "I guess I'm going to need to hire one of those people who organizes the lives of complete strangers and really get some help getting rid of more *stuff.*" She'd apologized for their couch several times and lamented over the fact that she and Rudolf hadn't taken the time to look for a new one.

It was obvious James had inherited his height from Mary Jane. She towered over her husband, Rudolf, who was a short, plump physicist with a mass of grayish-white hair that stuck up in peaks. *Didn't these people ever comb their hair?* I wondered. *And did they all get their glasses at the same discount store?*

I became fascinated by how little some people could care about appearance. I knew it wasn't necessarily a Mormon characteristic. Even though Cassie and Bud, according to Alex, were Mormons, Michelle Wilcox, whom I'd gotten to know through AP classes, always looked smashing, especially her hair. I wasn't sure at the time if Emma Smith Pratt in my geography class was Mormon or Quaker, but for the most part, the majority of Mormons I'd seen dressed modestly but stylishly.

I'd even seen a few Mormon missionaries with perfect haircuts, good-fitting suits, and lint brushes. If anything, the Tabernacle Choir members on television looked a bit *too* well-groomed, even a little stiff, but then most of them were old—in their forties, possibly.

No, the style problem was unique to the Wickenbees themselves. They were so involved in intellectual pursuits that they simply didn't bother themselves with certain other aspects of life that most people regarded as important. For instance, not only did Rudolf often wear mismatched socks, I once saw him start out of the house with a black loafer on one foot and a brown boot on the other. Luckily Mary Jane caught the oversight.

Other than some basics, such as keeping themselves and their clothing clean, James and his parents didn't seem concerned about other aspects of fashion. Details, such as what actually fit or matched, did not seem of importance to them. It was almost scary how well I was beginning to relate to and understand these people—except, of course, their affiliation with a church I considered abnormally strict and structured. Why the intellectual Wickenbees would belong to such a church remained a mystery. I finally risked bringing up the topic.

"So tell me this," I asked James one day as he studied the chessboard. "As bright as you are and as bright as all your family members seem to be, how on earth can you believe in something like the Mormon Church—or any religion, for that matter? Have you actually thought it through, or were you just born a Mormon and now it's, well, you know, a way of life for you."

James pushed his glasses up the bridge of his nose. "I completely believe in it."

"But why? I mean how can you? Science has refuted religion on almost every count."

"Scientists only believe in what they see and what is there before them. That changes from era to era. What we knew a hundred years ago is a pittance compared to what we know now. Most intelligent people acknowledge that what we know even today in our supposed enlightened era is just a microscopic grain of sand compared to all there is to know."

"Yes, but you don't mean to tell me that you believe in the creationist theory. How can you possibly believe that the world was created in seven days?"

"Six days," said James. "And time is not the same from an eternal standpoint. God's days aren't the same as ours."

"I see, and that's interesting. But are you telling me that you seriously believe that a supreme being created everything? What about the big bang theory? I can't understand how anyone could believe in a god. Where's your evidence?"

"The evidence is everywhere. I can't understand how anyone could *not* believe in God."

James started talking astronomy then, and physics and biology—how each related to religion, specifically the Mormon religion. He talked about the miracle of new cell growth and how each cell seemed to come with instructions that helped it instinctively know exactly who and what it was required to become. James claimed we were all created spiritually first in another existence.

"My stars, you really do believe this, don't you." I was in shock. An IQ of 185 and he was telling me about some type of heavenly Twilight Zone?

"I do," James said, peering at me again over his glasses. "In

38

fact, I have a book that theorizes how it all fits together. It's called *The Science and Religion Connection* and was written by a leader of our church. I'd be happy to loan it to you."

Uh-oh, I thought. *What have I begun?* "Um . . . no . . . no, thank you. I don't really need to read any literature on your church. I was just curious as to how you can believe something that isn't backed up by sound evidence." *Why on earth,* I wondered, *had I voluntarily ventured into this danger zone?* It was like jumping across a fence with a sign that says "Firing Range." I felt I should have known better.

"No evidence? There's evidence all around us. Do you really believe that everything needs to be scientifically proven first?" James was still very much engaged in the discussion. He'd pushed his glasses up three times in fifteen seconds.

"That's okay," I said, "I really don't want to get into this. I'm sorry I brought it up." I was anxious to move to another topic as quickly as possible.

But James wasn't ready to move on. "Truth is truth, no matter where you find it. I'll get you more information."

"Nooooo, thank you." I lifted my hand to indicate that this was where it ended and that I was there for one reason and one reason only—chess. How foolish I felt for having started this conversation. "I'm just not interested in any religion," I said quickly. *Or fictional hogwash,* I remember thinking to myself. "Forget I mentioned it. Let's just get back to our chess match."

That's the last time I'm going to give James Orville Wickenbee a foot in the door, I also remember thinking.

Chapter Seven

T he monitor almost directly above me is showing that Northwest Flight 107, which was on time when it stopped in St. Louis, is now twenty minutes behind schedule. James's first layover was in San Francisco, but apparently his plane must have taken off late from there. I'm highly relieved because I still don't feel ready to see my friend. Why? Why am I so *unprepared* to see James when I've known for two years this moment was coming?

Through the window I can see the flickering of planes arriving and taking off, each with a crew and passengers. Multiply the hundreds of flights that leave and land here at the Cleveland airport by the thousands of airports throughout the world and it adds up to an amazing number of planes flying around the skies. James and I once discussed how surprised the Wright brothers would be today if they could see where their experiments with "the flying machine" had led.

Even after traveling abroad several times—once with Uncle Bartho and Alex, twice with Mom, and once with Alex alone, I still go into panic mode at takeoff. I know it makes no sense, that statistically speaking the chances of getting injured or killed in a car accident are actually far greater than the chances of being in a plane crash, but there's something so—I don't know—*unnatural* about going up above the world and its buildings and everything here on earth.

From the reflections in the window to my right, I can see that several more people have arrived to meet James. Where are my glasses? I haven't worn glasses for years, but my eyes started giving me problems a couple of months ago and the optometrist said my contacts have scraped the outer layer of my corneas. In order for my eyes to heal, they'll need a good long rest. He advised me not to wear my contacts until the injury has cleared up completely. So where are those nasty things? Did I put my glasses case in the side pocket of my bag? I did! I click open the case, pull the out-of-style frames from it, slip them onto my nose, and peer through them.

I'm guessing it's Ruthie who's come in with the large, silver and blue balloon. Unfortunately glasses don't do that much good when a woman wearing a large poncho and carrying a tote bag the size of Canada is blocking your view. When she finally moves away, I see that it's my lovely aunt all right. Even with all the added weight around her middle—she's expecting her little girl any day— Ruthie still looks as chic as her husband doesn't. Not that I notice Phil's appearance that much anymore. What can I say? The man treats my aunt as if she's made of spun gold. I stopped caring what he looked like about the time I caught him gently and carefully painting Ruthie's toenails for her. And that was before she was expecting. "It's so awkward to paint your own toenails," Ruthie explained. It also became obvious within weeks that, just like his brother, there was much more to Phil than met the eye.

Maybe that's why it didn't bother me nearly as much as I thought it would when Ruthie made the decision to be baptized a member of the Mormon faith just two-and-a-half months after she and Phillip were married. We're only afraid of what we don't know and by that time I was already growing accustomed to these "peculiar"—as they call themselves—latter-day saints. Unlike me, Ruthie isn't a complex woman and life is far less complicated when a couple is unified in their beliefs.

Still I didn't want anyone getting the impression that *I* planned to be sucked in myself. "Nooooo, thank you," I had responded at the end of January when Mom asked if I planned to attend Ruthie's baptism. "I'm not interested in seeing people jumping up and down or rolling in the aisles."

Alex didn't find my comment that amusing. "What a clown," he said without smiling.

Mom, however, took my wisecrack in stride and joined in. "I think it's just the Mormon toddlers that jump up and down and roll in the aisles," she said dryly. "I don't believe the Mormon adults roll in the aisles."

"Ah!" I lifted my eyebrows and nodded into my coffee. But then I lowered my eyebrows and looked up from my cappuccino as I remembered that James and I always played chess on Saturday afternoon. "Just a minute now! What about our chess game? If

James is helping with this baptism, does that mean he isn't playing chess with me today?"

"Yes, let's keep our priorities straight here," said Alex.

Mom hopped around a little as she attempted to slip her shoe strap back onto her heel. "Oh, that's right. James left you a message that your game is still on. He said to come over at the usual time but that he'd just need to quit a little early so he can get ready."

"The way *he* dresses, it should only take him fourteen, possibly fifteen seconds to get himself pulled together," I quipped. But as I took a careful sip of my coffee, I felt happily relieved. I honestly wasn't sure I could survive the week without my Saturday chess match with James. "So I take it *you're* going to the baptism," I said to Alex. My brother had worn a tie probably twice before in his life and he seemed to be having some trouble knotting this one.

"Sure." He eyed me warily. "Trust me. It'll be fine."

"Sure," I repeated, getting up to help him with the final twist and loop through. *I trust you, Alex, but be careful,* I thought, hoping that no one from Fairport would see him go into the Mormon building.

In spite of his choice of unusual and out-of-the-mainstream friends, Alex was surprisingly popular with the general school populace and things were looking good for him. But I was fearful that just one rumor about him *doing* something unusual and out of the mainstream, well, like putting on a tie and going to this baptism, would be enough to cause a whisper campaign that would fling him into oblivion.

It didn't take much to get flung. The most qualified candidate for president in our junior high, Ed Parrin, had been a shoo-in until somebody found out that he attended operas and was taking singing lessons. Some of the smart alecks and jocks had had a field day with that. They sang fake arias to him in the halls and tormented him nonstop. Ed not only lost the election, but finally found life among the Roosevelt Raptors so unbearable that he transferred to Lincoln Junior High and became a Hedgehog.

Further, there was Lyla Fannen to worry about. I considered it nothing short of a miracle that Lyla and several of her Lyla-nites, as Alex called them, were even still with us at our lunch table. When the new semester had started, Sonja had had to switch to first lunch and had been replaced with Melinda Challister, who pretty much wore only Paul van Eckstein clothing and had her hair cut by my stylist: Raphael. Luckily Adriana had our lunch now as well and gave me the fortitude to deal with Lyla and Dolly.

While Mom and Alex were at the baptism, I looked through a couple of magazines and then perused the *Wall Street Journal*. When I finally closed the paper, I noticed that either Alex or Mom had left a copy of the Book of Mormon on the coffee table. Without picking it up, I flipped through the first few pages, stopping at an introductory page where some "witnesses" testified they had seen an angel. "Oh please," I whispered to myself. I shut the book quickly when I heard the garage door open.

"So how was it?" I asked Mom and Alex with sufficient casualness.

"To be honest with you," Mom said, "I was a little nervous about what to expect. But I was very impressed. It was a beautiful meeting and there was nothing strange about it. Not even any rolling in the aisles," she added facetiously, tipping her head at me—"nothing out of the ordinary." Then she paused. "I guess the only thing I can think of that seemed unusual is that the parishioners presented the program instead of the pastor. Isn't a pastor paid to do that kind of thing? But then, let's see, he's called a bishop in the LDS faith. There were several bishops there—three or four backups."

"LDS bishops don't get paid," Alex informed us. "In fact, a bishop never quits his day job, and he runs things mostly at night and on weekends."

"It's unusual to see unpaid volunteer clergy, but I think that's wonderful," my mother said. It wasn't a surprising thing for my mother to say. She was practically a full-time volunteer herself. She was on the Fairport Beautification Committee, the Friends of Flora and Fauna, the Reaching out for Literacy Program, and about three or four cultural and art boards whose names I could never keep straight. It was her charity league that she got the most excited about.

"James gave an inspiring talk about the Holy Ghost," my mother continued. "He explained beautifully how the Mormons view the trinity. Let's see, what did he say, Alex—that they are one in purpose, but otherwise separate?"

"That's right," Alex said.

"James spoke?" That caught my interest. He seemed awfully young to be considered capable of speaking at such an important function.

"Yes, James is a fine speaker. It was an inspirational, beautiful, and well thought out talk."

I was suspicious now. *A talk probably designed to recruit the non-members there,* I speculated. It was one thing for Ruthie to join, but I certainly didn't want Phillip or James swooping in on my mother and Alex. It bothered me a great deal that Alex was suddenly acting as though he were some kind of expert on Mormons and Mormonism.

"I didn't realize the Holy Ghost had so many functions," Mom continued. "Maybe I just hadn't thought that much about this *personage* as the Mormons refer to him. James said that the Holy Spirit is the mediator between us and the Lord." Mom continued reviewing James's talk with such energy that it was really beginning to concern me. But then I'd been concerned for some time about the Wickenbees' influence on my mother and Alex.

"It made a lot of sense," added Alex soberly. "Haven't you ever felt a warm feeling inside when something sounded right?" Alex had that puppy dog look in his eyes he sometimes gets, which really made me nervous. I rolled up the latest *Times* and pointed it at him. "Don't you dare tell me you're getting caught up in this emotional nonsense," I said. "It's fine for Ruthie. Maybe she even needed it. But you still have your life ahead of you, Alex."

"All I'm saying is that we've all felt that way," Alex responded. "Who's to say feelings like that aren't from a heavenly source? I just know I've felt that warm feeling before, and I felt it again today."

I came unglued. "You two are *not* going to let yourselves be duped into any religious foolishness. I don't want to hear any more about some kind of ghost. You're home now and away from la-la church-land. It's time to tune back into reality and the real world! I mean it! Here, let's watch some television." I pushed the remote power button on our television just in time to see a woman lowering herself into a container of cockroaches. Quickly I switched to the nature channel where some lions were devouring an antelope. "See!" I said, my eyes stretched. "Great entertainment! Yes, let's get your minds on something worthwhile."

Chapter Eight

It wasn't until the last week of February that I figured out why Lyla was still at our lunch table when people who weren't even jotted in the margins of Fairport's social register continued to gather there. One day I caught her gazing at my brother over her croissant, a small, lovesick, half-smile on her face. Lyla liked Alex! As hard as it is to understand now, I was ecstatic at what I considered an astounding and fortuitous development! Then I decided that maybe it wasn't that astounding. Alex was probably the only male in the school who didn't fall at her feet in a heap, muttering incoherently when she so much as smiled at him.

I couldn't wait to tell my brother. "I have some great news for you! Lyla Fannen *likes* you," I let him know that afternoon when I found him in the back shooting baskets.

"Not interested," Alex tossed over his shoulder as he aimed the ball toward the hoop.

"You're not interested?" I followed him to the other side of the court as he retrieved the ball, my breath visible in the icy air. "Do you realize how many *dudes,* as you call them, would like to be in your place?"

He didn't answer but made a shot from well behind the free-throw line.

"Hundreds," I answered.

"Uh-huh." Alex glanced at his watch, tossed the ball into the large bin under our apple tree, and hurried to the back door. I followed my brother into the kitchen, rubbing my hands together to warm them. Alex flipped open the pantry and began scouring the shelves for on-the-go junk food.

"Playing hard-to-get has worked so far, but if you don't start tossing out some morsels of encouragement—or if Lyla starts feeling that you never will—she'll, well, get discouraged," I said. "Maybe you should sit a little closer to her during lunch tomorrow. And when we start planning our birthday party—I'm thinking something big—we should make sure she and her friends are invited."

"I like where I sit." Alex shrugged. "And I'm thinking a *small* party with *real* friends."

I formed a fist, digging my nails into my palm, then stretched my hand and patted it into the air. "Alex, believe me, Lyla's not going to put up with the way you treat her forever. She'll get discouraged."

"Discouraged" wasn't the right word really. "Disappointed" was a better word. And a disappointed Lyla Fannen would not a pretty picture make. Oh no. "So far you haven't said more than two or three words to her. On the other hand," I continued, "when

James and his little friends come around, words come spewing out of you like Fourth of July fireworks. Why are you so nice to *those people,* and so snobby to the . . ." I hesitated.

"The snobby?" asked Alex.

"Okay, yes." Now *he* was categorizing people, but I didn't call him on it. "Do you realize how lucky we are that Lyla and her friends are still with us considering that James Orville is forever bringing the school's strangest possible people to our table? It's bad enough that he's there himself." I blinked a few times, knowing full well how Alex would react to my statement. When I tried to make it sound better, it actually sounded worse. "It says something about Lyla that someone of her social stature is willing to be seen with James and his friends just so she can be around you, and okay, maybe me and Adriana as well, but mostly you. This is a sacrifice on her part."

Alex lifted the bottle of Gatorade he'd found in the refrigerator, took a swig of it, and then said, "And that's why I don't think she's someone I'd be interested in getting to know better. Thanks for putting it into words for me!"

"Alex, we're talking about Lyla Fannen!" I looked for something to throw at him and settled on a soggy sponge that our latest kitchen helper hadn't bothered to put away. "Can't you, just for once, not spend all your time talking to people who aren't going to get you anywhere?" Yes, I actually said those words.

"You mean people like James?"

I paused. "Well . . . you and I know James is okay but . . ."

"Just okay?"

He and I both knew that James was *much* better than okay so I relented. "All right, you're right, he's a great guy—interesting and fun to talk to—but that becomes a little beside the point when he . . . Alex, *look* at him. We've talked about this before." But I hadn't felt this guilty before. Why did I feel like I'd stabbed a good friend in the back? Was it because I just had? On the other hand, my brother was my primary concern, I told myself. "It's just that he's . . . you know! You *know* what people who don't know James think of him."

"*You're* the dork," said Alex, aiming the sponge right back at me. It hit my new denim jacket. I grabbed a clean dishtowel, narrowed my eyes and sighed with disgust at my brother's stubbornness. Couldn't he just for once cooperate?

Chapter Nine

I realized that maybe it was good Alex wasn't a yes-man two days later when we received a phone call from Lyla.

"Oh, hi, Lyla," I said, trying not to sound too astounded. It was a known fact that Lyla rarely called people. They called her.

"I'm having a little get-together tonight and wondered if you and Alex would like to drop by," Lyla said, her words slightly slurred. "In fact, why don't you put Alex on and I'll ask him myself."

"Sure. You bet." I turned to Alex with a don't-blow-this expression. "Alex, it's Lyla Fannen."

Alex frowned and knotted his eyebrows. "What does *she* want?"

"I told you she likes you," I whispered, my hand blocking the sound from the phone. I was trying really hard not to let Alex see how excited I was at this new development. Never mind that it sounded like Lyla had taken a little something from her parents' liquor cabinet.

Alex rolled his eyes but held out his hand for the phone. "Alex speaking," he said formally. I was peeved he wasn't acting more friendly. He could have at least acknowledged her by name. I didn't want to leave the kitchen so I busied myself with the things in the dishwasher, all the while listening carefully.

"Sure, if I can bring a few friends." Alex looked in my direction with a mischievous smile.

I gave him a disgusted expression, shaking my head.

"Oh, I'm thinking Cassie, Terrance, James. You know, that group."

I sunk into myself and sighed. *What was Alex doing?* I wondered.

"Well, in that case I'll politely decline, as they say." Alex shifted the phone to his other ear. "Oh, I think I understand." The next pause was longer. My brother's eye twitched and he thinned his mouth into a sharp line. Alex turned his back to me and walked toward the dining room. Luckily, I take after Mom when it comes to the ability to hear. "Just you and me, huh?" he said quietly. Alex glanced in my direction. "No, she's not acting like she's listening." Alex lowered his head and thrust his chin forward. "Uh-huh, I think I understand. . . . Think about it? I don't even think that's necessary."

After another long pause, I heard, "Wait, I don't think you understand, Lyla. I don't need to think about it because I already know that I'm going to have to turn down your offer. . . . That's right. Uh-huh. Look, why don't you get yourself a cup of coffee or something and sober up? I'm not sure you're yourself today. . . . Yes, that is what I said."

Lyla apparently wasn't believing what she was hearing. I'm sure she wasn't expecting this level of resistance, or *any* level of resistance. What had she offered?

"Oh, no, I don't think I'll be changing my mind," said my brother. "Not now. Not ever."

I shut my eyes. "Okay, what was that about?" I said, my voice tired. "Did she ask you out or something?"

"You don't want to know," Alex said, hanging up the phone.

I widened my eyes and began to stutter. "Oh, well . . . seriously? Are you sure that's what she meant?"

"Oh, yeah."

"Well, you did the right thing then, but . . ."

"But what?"

"Well, couldn't you have played along for a little while longer?" It's still hard to believe that's what I said.

"Why would I do that?" Alex stared at me in disbelief.

"Because who knows what's going to happen now."

"I don't really care what happens now, Jana."

Alex amazed me sometimes. I could have named quite a number of classmates who would have jumped at what Lyla had offered. In fact, I couldn't think of many who wouldn't. But the truth is I admired Alex for what he said to Lyla and always will. Even though I couldn't very well ask him to be less than he is, however, I still found myself wishing he'd been more diplomatic. Lyla had just been bashed royally and I was fearful about what she'd do next. Very fearful.

"She's going to be soooooo unhappy," I said to my brother.

— ∞ —

What Lyla did next surprised both Alex and me completely. Apparently she wasn't one to give up easily. I saw her in the hall the next day between third and fourth, running her manicured index finger around the top button of Alex's shirt. I pulled to a halt, readjusted my books, and turned toward the drinking fountain. When I saw her sashay away, I hurried toward Alex to find out what she'd said.

"Just that she's sorry," he replied. "She said she had a little too much cough medication yesterday and that she hoped I wasn't angry with her. She said to stop by her house and she'd fix me a drink and a little something to eat to apologize."

"What did you say?"

"I told her I don't drink and that that wasn't necessary."

"Not even a 'maybe sometime'?"

"Not even a 'maybe sometime.'"

I'm not sure how many more times Lyla made plays for my brother those next few days and how many times he not so politely declined. When would she catch on? I was guessing it wouldn't be long. Sure enough, it wasn't.

Maybe it was the angle Lyla had her head cocked that lunch period or maybe it was the extra lift of her eyebrow that tipped me off. I'd known for some time that Lyla would eventually realize that Alex was not and never would be interested in her, and now I recognized that that time was here. We were going to see the real Lyla now and it wasn't going to be pretty.

I nervously followed her gaze and saw that she was staring at

James in what I called his Shirt of Many Colors. Not only was her eyebrow lifted, but one corner of her mouth was curled in a poisonous smile. James's shirt was a country-western number with patches of bright patterns. It was the strangest shirt he owned and that was saying something. And, as was the case with most of his clothes, it didn't fit him properly. I made a few comments trying to get Lyla sidetracked, but like a cobra focused on its prey, she was concentrating on James and James alone.

Finally, after he and Alex had stopped talking and the two were contentedly eating the homemade sandwiches James made for both of them now, Lyla struck. "Wherever did you find that interesting shirt, James? Was it handmade in Idaho?"

James, who was just lifting his sandwich for another bite, set it back down and smiled at Lyla contentedly. If he was aware of the sarcasm in her voice, he wasn't letting on. "Yes, I guess you could say it was," he said congenially. "Thanks for asking. My Great-Grandmother Ingebritt made it for me." But then James studied the front of the shirt more carefully. "On second thought, I think this is the one she made for my brother Felix. Mine was a little brighter, but I got phosphate on it."

"Phosphate, oh dear." Lyla scratched the corner of her mouth with her carefully manicured pinky fingernail. "What's that? Some kind of manure?"

"Well, no, but manure *does* often contain phosphate."

"How interesting. You *must* give us all an in-depth report on manure one of these days. But you say this other shirt was even brighter?"

Did James have any clue about what was happening? It was

spring-water clear to me that Lyla had given up and was apparently planning to take out her anger at Alex's rejection on poor James. Thumbing her nose at him was going to be her way of letting us know she was finished with us. Or was she just getting started? I was pretty sure I didn't want to know. I just wanted James removed from this mortifying situation. I wanted us all away from Lyla and our lunch table and maybe even our school because I was highly aware of Lyla's *modus operandi* by then.

Lyla pulled her beautifully formed lips into a smirk. "And you say your brother's name is Felix?" she asked, smiling at Dolly who seemed uncertain about whether to smile back.

I jumped in and began paddling because I really did not want James to embarrass himself further by announcing that Felix was on an LDS mission. "James has a big family," I said. "He has five brothers and two sisters. Isn't that right, James?"

"Wow!" said Lyla. "Eight children in the family?"

I blinked. What had I done?

"My brothers Fred and Felix—" James tried to continue.

"Felix is just older than James," I explained quickly.

"And I'm guessing quite a bit shorter," Lyla said, lifting her arm and encircling her wrist with her manicured index finger and thumb, then sliding them upward to indicate she was referring to the large portion of James's wrist that wasn't covered by the sleeve of his brother's shirt. "So is this older, shorter Felix home on the potato farm in Idaho?"

I looked from Lyla to James. It was useless. I knew James would be delighted to tell Lyla where his brother was. Things began moving in slow motion.

"Felix is in Brazil," James said happily. "On a mission for our church. And my brother Fred is serving a mission in Argentina."

I readjusted myself in my chair and silently popped my lips at Adriana.

"How interesting!" said Lyla. This was a double-eyebrow-lift revelation, and Lyla glanced over at Dolly again, at Melinda, and then back at James. "Don't tell me you're *Mormons?*" I could tell she was thrilled at this new and unexpected tidbit of information.

"Some people call us that, but it's not the official name. Our church is called The Church of Jesus Christ of Latter-day Saints," said James without apology.

"Uh-huh. Uh-huh," Lyla nodded, her mouth open. "I see."

"*Mormon* is just a nickname," Alex chipped in.

Stay out of this, Alex, I thought. *Don't even stick in a toe.*

It was too late. Lyla turned in Alex's direction. "And how do you know so much about this, Alex?" She was practically hissing with glee. "Are you planning to join the Mormon church too? Are you planning to give up partying for praying? Gosh, maybe you already have! That would explain a few things." Lyla chortled at her cleverness.

Alex just smiled. "Well, you never know."

"Oh, wow!" Lyla was having a wonderful time. "Or *wowsers* as your little friend Cassie puts it." She turned to me. "And are you planning to join too, Jana? Maybe you could all move to Idaho and start a potato farm. You could get matching shirts." Lyla smirked at her friends.

Melinda smiled nervously at Lyla and then at me. Dolly picked at her salad with her fork.

"So, Jana," Lyla lowered her voice in a confidential tone, "is there something going on between you and James that we need to know about? Something we should announce in the *Fairport Gazette?*"

I didn't answer because I was still staring at Alex, concerned about how he'd answered when Lyla asked him if he was planning to join the Mormon church.

"Jana? I asked you a question."

"Oh . . . what?" Lyla mistook my loss of focus as fear.

"I asked if this is just an Alex-thing or if you and James are bestest friends too? . . . Or are you two . . . you know?"

"James and I play chess together."

"You play what?" she laughed a little and smiled a crooked smile at her friends, her eyebrows again lifted.

It's a funny thing with anger—sometimes it begins slowly and gradually festers until you either need to water it down or allow it to erupt. Other times it comes quickly and you either explode or you rein it in and control it and use it. In debate my sophomore year, anger helped me choose words that struck hard and with impact. Right now I suddenly no longer cared about all the effort it had taken to get Lyla at our table and all the hours of brown-nosing that was just about to be blown out the window.

"Chess," I said to Lyla, facing her now, the phony social veneer no longer lubricating my voice. "James and I have gotten to know each other, and yes, we've become friends because we play chess together. And no, I'm not studying his religion or him, I'm just studying chess." I said the words calmly.

"Chess, you say? Oh my." She smiled again at her friends.

I really was not appreciating Lyla's efforts to ridicule my brother and my friend and me. Further, making fun of chess was like mocking Uncle Bartho, and *nobody* could get away with that. I was feeling outright hostility toward Lyla Fannen now. And a hostile Jana did not a pretty picture make.

"Yes, Lyla," I responded patiently. "James and I play chess. That's c-h-e-s-s." Even as I was spelling it for her, I knew that I was giving her information she could use against me—information she could grab onto and fly around the school like a kite. Gathering information about people was her hobby.

No, playing chess wasn't any stranger than attending operas or taking singing lessons, but in the wrong hands anything could be made to appear strange and unacceptable. Playing chess was not quite the same as belonging to a strict church that didn't allow even an occasional cappuccino, but Lyla, I was sure, would find a way to use it against me. Oh, I'd seen and heard her in action. If she couldn't use the overly religious angle, Lyla would be happy to go for the overly intellectual angle. And that's exactly what she did.

"My aren't we bright!" Lyla smiled over at Dolly, who was nervously adjusting her skintight shirt. It had all happened so suddenly that I think it was news to Dolly and Melinda that we weren't all friends anymore. Lyla tipped her head at Adriana who looked down at her soup.

Lyla returned her gaze to me. "I can just see you and James sitting for hours, Jana, staring at the chessboard . . . *and* at each other," Lyla continued, a lilt in her voice.

Possibly because I was studying my peach low-fat yogurt and

not looking at her, Lyla thought she had already won, that it was all over and she'd, so to speak, just checkmated my king. But Lyla had gone too far with her taunting. With a cold smile, I stared her down. "You know, you're right, Lyla. Not many people here at Fairport are into chess like James and I are. Most students here really aren't that into anything that might require a few brain cells. I'd say the majority of Fairport students don't know the difference between a neuron and a neutron. Certain people in this school have approximately the same IQ as their Louis Vuitton handbags. When it comes to emotional IQ and maturity, they're even lower. And when it comes to moral principles of any kind they're scraping lake bottom."

Lyla opened her mouth but nothing came out. It was a satisfying moment.

The next day, Lyla, her Louis Vuitton bag, and her other accessories—Melinda and Dolly—were no longer at our lunch table. They'd moved to the table with Carson Parker and Dan Ravino, the most popular preps, and even a few athletes.

Dolly kept looking back over at our table, apparently confused and undoubtedly concerned about what had happened. This seemed to annoy Lyla, who at one point took hold of one of Dolly's white-blonde curls and jerked her face away from us. Then Lyla whispered something to the others as she sneered at us. Soon all the people at her table and a few at the next were looking over and laughing.

I sighed into my carton of raspberry low-fat yogurt. The satisfaction of stinging Lyla had worn off and I was already regretting what I'd done. My quick tongue had more than likely just cost

Alex the school presidency. And I'd criticized Alex for his lack of diplomacy? Still, I marveled at Lyla's timing. That very Friday, our birthday no less, all candidates wishing to run for school office had been asked to meet in the library to register. Lyla couldn't have dumped us at a worse, or from her perspective, I suppose, a better time.

I apologized to Alex that night. "I guess we'll be having that small birthday party after all. And I guess there's no point having you sign up to run for president of the school."

"It's okay, Jana, because like I've told you about four thousand times, I'm not running for an office anyway."

"I suppose we could assess our losses," I suggested, "and go for what's feasible now. Maybe you won't make president without the queen of the school's blessings, but you don't need nearly as many votes to be elected as a school senator. You could probably even get in with just the dork and geek votes alone." I knew I had probably once again offended him with my harsh wording, and I blinked a little, but my concern was quickly overshadowed by the excitement that was flooding back at what I saw as a real possibility. "In fact, I'll bet you *could* make the school senate."

"Dork and geek votes, huh?" Alex hit the remote channel button three times in a row before he looked up at me. "Look, since you like to label people and place them in groups, put me in with the group who is not interested in earning votes of any kind. In fact, I have a question: Could you finally let it go!?"

I wouldn't. I *couldn't* let it go, so I used Mom's psychology. "Well, I guess it's up to you."

"That's right, it is."

"Fine."

"Fine."

"Okay."

"Okay."

"Fine."

"Fine."

"We said that," I said, trying to diffuse the tension.

Alex sat up and leaned forward, his eyes bulging. "I mean it! Listen carefully. Once and for all, I am *not* running. Do . . . you . . . understand?"

"I suppose so." I was nervous now. When Alex's eyes start bulging, it generally means negotiations are over.

"Good, because I really DO NOT—and I'm saying these words loudly because you seem to be having some problem registering what I'm saying—I repeat: I DO NOT want to hear ANYMORE about my running for an office."

"Fine."

"Fine." He shook his head. "FINE!"

I sighed and plopped down on the floor in the corner in disappointment. All this time I'd been sure my brother was just being coy and that he'd eventually acquiesce. Or maybe I had just been trying to convince myself that I believed he was being coy and would come around. Maybe I'd really known all along that he wasn't interested. Maybe I'd thought that my wanting it for him badly enough would eventually override his reticence and that my urgency would make up for his lack of enthusiasm. But Alex it appeared, truly and honestly was not interested in running for a school office. I realized now that I was just going to have to acknowledge that fact.

Strangely, after a few minutes, however, something I recognized as relief was seeping into my psyche. If there was really absolutely nothing I could do to convince Alex to enter the race, and Alex honestly was not going to run for a high school office of any kind, the pressure, I realized, was completely off me too. Even though Lyla was out of the picture, there were other people I'd been thinking I'd still need to brownnose and I was getting tired, very tired of brownnosing.

"At least I won't need to kiss any more skinny little you-know-whats," I mumbled loudly enough for Alex to hear.

My brother allowed a small laugh to escape. "Yeah, that really wasn't like you." I think he too was relieved. I think he thought I was finally letting go of my ambitions for him. It was only partially true.

I'd pretty much abandoned the high school office idea, but I still had plenty of ambition for Alex when it came to a post-high school career. In fact, I was at that very moment thinking beyond high school to college. If Alex could get into a good law school, he'd easily be able to move from law into politics. And wouldn't Lyla and her lovely friends be clamoring to claim his friendship when my brother was governor of Ohio or even a congressman? Oh boy, would they ever be claiming him as their very *bestest* friend then! But that brought up another concern.

"So you were kidding about what you said about joining the Church of Jesus Christ of LDS, weren't you?"

"I'm taking lessons over at James's house," Alex said, "on

Tuesdays. I've been wanting to tell you about it. So far it's pretty good stuff. Makes a lot of sense."

"What!" I scrambled out of the corner. This time *my* eyes were bulging. "I thought you were playing chess on Tuesdays! What are you telling me? Are you *serious?*"

"I'm not serious about anything right now. I just said I was studying this and that it seems to make sense."

"Well, I certainly hope you're not seriously considering making any kind of a commitment because if you join the LDS faith you might as well kiss any kind of a political career good-bye. You leave the accepted conventional Protestant churches and you just don't make it in this world, my dear brother. You might as well just start growing potatoes in the backyard!" But it was a huge mistake to bring politics up again just minutes after he'd let me know so emphatically that it wasn't on his agenda.

"Good grief!" Alex shouted. "I feel like there's some kind of a barnacle attached to me! What's it going to take, Jana, to convince you that I don't want to be in politics *ever*—not even after high school! I thought I told you that. I want to teach math or history someday and help kids get a grip on life. And what makes you think being a Mormon would stop anyone from achieving his political goals anyway? Being Mormon might even help. Maybe people would enjoy seeing some politicians in office with morals for a change. But even if I joined the Mormon faith—which is unlikely—it would never be *me* running for a political office, okay? It won't, and I repeat, *won't* ever be me. I don't know why you won't believe that and give it up! If you want one of us to run for a political office so badly, why don't you go run yourself!"

There was a long pause. "Because you've seen *my* people skills," I finally muttered.

Alex didn't want to laugh at that—he tried hard not to—but he did anyway. In any event by putting me on the defensive, he'd skillfully diverted my attention from what I considered the main concern: that he would even be looking into the Mormon faith.

— හ —

Two days later Alex and I celebrated our birthday *quietly*—that is if you can call anything Cassie invites herself to as *quiet*. Our family members stopped by; Ruthie brought balloons. While people visited, James taught our little cousin Reggie the names of several of the chess pieces and kept him happily occupied for a good fifteen minutes. Later Adriana and Butch and Paul stopped by.

"Lyla's having a huge party tonight at her house," Adriana was kind enough to let us know. "Practically the whole school's there—well, those she figures *count*. Would you believe *I* got invited? I stopped by there for a minute or two just to see what was gong on."

"Yeah, we went over for a while too," Butch added sheepishly.

I nodded and turned to my brother. "Gosh, Alex," I said sarcastically. "I told Lyla our birthday was coming up so she must be having this party to celebrate. I guess she just kind of forgot to tell *us* about it."

"No doubt," said my brother as he played along. He scooped up Reggie and lifted him to his shoulders. "A surprise party. Surprise! You're not invited!"

I tried to laugh as I nodded, but I could feel the prickling sensation of tears behind my eyes, and then I had to swallow.

Chapter Ten

ᴏᴑᴅ

T he older, gray-haired gentleman who just walked up to the Hertz car rental booth here at the airport looks so much like Uncle Bartholomew that I'm fishing for my glasses again. I'm not sure why I'm bothering, when of course it isn't Uncle Bartho.

What I wouldn't give if I could walk up to that man and he really was Uncle Bartho. For a year or so right after my uncle died, I missed him so much that sometimes I imagined I *did* see him. "Hey Uncle Bartho, you've heard of Elvis sightings," I joked, because when I was alone in my room I still talked to him. "Well, I have Bartho sightings." Our uncle loved a good joke and I think he would have laughed heartily at that if he could have.

"Uncle Bartho was *my* savior," I remember telling Alex one day in ninth grade when we were debating religion. Even before we met James, and even before Alex attended any church, my brother had considered himself a Christian.

"Well, he's not *the* savior, but Old Bartho sure pulled us out of a mess," Alex agreed. "I think God inspired him to fly in that day."

"I think he came because he loved us and *sensed* something was wrong," I said.

"Same thing," said Alex.

And then I didn't want to discuss it anymore. All I knew then and now is that for whatever reason Bartho came, it was extremely fortunate he did. Things couldn't have been much worse. After our father decided to abandon us in order to pursue his personal dreams, which included gambling away even our college funds, our sweet old uncle virtually rescued us from financial doom, its accompanying social humiliation, and even significant danger.

Mom basically fell apart after Dad left. In layman terms she had what's called a nervous breakdown. Dr. Griffin, my therapist, told me later that there's technically no such thing and that the term is misleading. I'm not sure about the "nervous" part of the term, but the "breakdown" part sounded to me like a perfectly accurate description.

It's amazing how fast things can slide downhill once they start moving in that direction. Yes, they say you never need to *look* poor, and I've learned since that you can find vintage clothing at flea markets and secondhand stores if you know where to look. Even these days I shop at consignment shops once in a while—not because I need to anymore, but because they don't make things with the quality and the workmanship they once did.

But I was barely thirteen then and I didn't know that such a thing as a quality secondhand store even existed. On the other hand, even secondhand stores would have declined our maxed-out credit cards. Not that it would have mattered what I wore. I could have worn a five-thousand-dollar Carolina Herrera dress and I would still have looked bad. As if things needed to get worse, not long after Dad left I immediately entered the portals of that infamous "awkward" stage. I grew five inches almost overnight; my complexion turned to dotted Swiss; and I was in need of some major dental work.

My mental and emotional state was in even worse shape than my appearance. Mom had begged Alex and me not to tell anyone what was happening. I might have turned to my aunts anyway had they even been living in the country, but Ruthie was in Europe at the time with Flashy Floyd, her nightmare of an ex, and Nadine and Charles were still in Brazil. I tried the best I could to pull together the pieces and play the role of adult, but I lacked the experience and the tools required.

Eighth graders have a way of finding out things, though, and soon word got around that our family had been booted out of our home and we were living in a seedy motel and that our mother had had a meltdown. Alex had a little easier time of it. His naturally positive "Things are going to get better" attitude helped him remain in fairly decent shape. Of course, Alex was never actually hungry. He had *friends,* and they *fed* him. Sometimes he ate at their houses and other times they shared a pizza or a sandwich with him. He'd wrap the leftovers in a napkin and bring home whatever he could, but there was never enough.

I'm pretty sure Alex never fully realized how bad things really were. I was the one who opened the mail, looked through Mom's papers, and made the phone calls. I was the one who conned free food from the Giant Eagle and made promises I knew I couldn't keep to the motel manager.

Needless to say it was a tremendous relief when Uncle Bartho showed up. The sweet old man packed us up immediately. I think he'd already seen the vermin hanging around outside. "You're outta here!" he said. I'd never heard words that thrilled me more. He moved us into a decent place in a good neighborhood and immediately got Mom psychiatric help. Then he had his secretary schedule appointments for me with a dermatologist, an orthodontist, and an optometrist. He also registered me into the Cotillion, one of Cleveland's finest finishing schools. Best of all, he bought us groceries.

Every time he came to town Bartho would drop by the nice, almost new, condo he'd leased for us to see how we were doing. Talking around the big cigar in his mouth, he'd say, "Know any kids 'round here who might want to go to a Cavaliers' game?" or "Who wants to take in a movie?" He took us to *Les Mis* for our birthday. "You have pretty good taste, Missy," he said to me after a shopping spree. "Maybe you'll become a fashion buyer or designer."

"I think I can do better than that," I told him. It must have sounded pretty arrogant coming from somebody he'd basically just hauled out of the trash, but Bartho seemed amused by my attitude. I quite often amused him. What can I say? He liked me.

"I'm guessing you could be just about anything you set out to be," he told me. Yes, the dear old man did his best to salvage my ego as well. And Mom's.

After she was feeling better, Uncle Bartho helped our mother land a decent job with an affiliate of Harper and Row publishing. It was well-paying work she loved with good benefits and a nice atmosphere. Thanks to her talent not only with syntax but also with people, Mom began advancing almost immediately. "I don't know how we're ever going to repay you, Bartho," I heard her tell him one night.

"You don't need to repay me," Uncle Bartho answered. "I'm your brother." His next words are still etched on my soul, "And you know how crazy I am about those kids of yours. I couldn't love them more if they were my own."

Then on a normal everyday Thursday afternoon, Uncle Bartho suffered a heart attack, just like that. His gardener rushed him to the emergency room at the nearest hospital and called us from there. We booked a flight immediately and hurried into the surgery ward only to discover we were too late. I'll never forget the doctor's mouth forming the words, "We're sorry, but he didn't make it."

Dr. Lancaster explained to us that three of Uncle Bartho's arteries had become blocked. He drew a diagram for us so that we would understand. Only we didn't understand. How could our uncle who was so necessary and dear to us suddenly be gone? He hadn't even said good-bye.

I took on the responsibility of informing the other family members of Uncle Bartho's death. After getting a hold of them, I discovered that Alex and Mom and I weren't the only ones Uncle Bartho had helped through some challenging times. He'd been in the process of helping Ruthie break free of her nasty marital mess, and he'd bailed out Nadine's family right after her husband's printing business went under.

But even in death, Uncle Bartho did not abandon us. There was no red tape and no waiting to receive our inheritance. He'd put everything in a trust fund and we were immediately provided for financially. It was a good feeling to know we had enough to live well, a decent car we could count on, and even a sound system that worked. But we didn't have *him*.

As I analyze it now, I wonder if part of the reason I was so intent on getting Alex involved in politics was because Uncle Bartho had specifically mentioned that as a good possibility for my brother. Maybe I felt that if I could get Alex to run for an office, I'd be honoring our sweet old uncle's wishes. On the other hand, maybe Alex was right. Maybe my intent was much more self-centered than that. Maybe I hoped that if Alex made it to the top that as his twin I'd automatically be hoisted up there as well.

That week of our birthday, I had no choice but to come to the conclusion that no matter how much I wanted Alex's political career to blossom, it just wasn't important to the one person it needed to be important to: Alex. He didn't plan to run for anything, not now, not ever. And well, ultimately it was up to him, not me. I knew Alex well enough to know you could only push him so far and then he'd start coming at you in reverse. It was disappointing, yes, but life, as I'd already discovered, was often disappointing. To Alex's relief, on the night of our birthday, I let him know that I finally accepted his decision.

The next day, however, my brother shared some news that threw me into a complete tailspin.

Chapter Eleven

Y ou heard me right. James is running for president of
Fairport," Alex said. "He told me last night."

"Has he lost his mind?" I felt as if somebody had just
kickboxed me in the stomach.

"Nope, he definitely still has it."

"Well, apparently, he doesn't." I pulled myself forward in the
leather chair where I had once again been reading. "I can't believe
James would do something that ridiculous." But then, with great
clarity and discomfort, I realized that I *could* see it. While amazingly bright in some ways, James was naïve, innocent, and completely idealistic in others. Panic set in. "Alex, you need to talk him
out of this and the sooner the better. You and I know that James
will be shark bait if he tries to run for president. He'll be eaten
alive." Alex had to know what I meant. With Lyla and her groupies
at Fairport's helm, students had become about as compassionate
as great whites.

"Don't think I didn't try. He's pretty committed." Alex pulled a piece of toast out of the toaster, flipped a knife from the drawer, and reached for the peanut butter. "He signed up at that meeting yesterday."

"But why? Why would he do something so self-destructive?" And how, I wondered, could Alex be going about his ordinary life, spreading peanut butter on toast, at a time like this?

"He says he doesn't like the direction things are heading at Fairport."

"That sounds like him." Rather than "Is it smart?" James's first question was always, "Is it right?"

"Hey, we should be glad. Look at it this way. Somebody's running who actually has some principles." My brother took a large bite of his toast, then grabbed a napkin from the napkin holder.

"He'll need a lot more than principles to survive something like this," I said, astounded that Alex was taking all this so lightly. I pulled my denim jacket from the back of the kitchen chair, grabbed my coffee cup and practically slammed it into the dishwasher. It was only two in the afternoon and an hour too early for my Saturday chess date with James, but I needed to get over to his house and I needed to get there fast! "Maybe you're going to stand there acting as if this is nothing, but I'm heading to James's right now," I told my brother. "This is an emergency!"

"Wait, I'll go with you." Alex calmly folded the remainder of his toast in half, wrapped it in the napkin, then pulled his Cleveland Indians cap from the pantry handle. "I promised James we'd powwow before you two start your chess game today."

"Powwow about what?"

"Ummm . . ." Alex left his fingers pressed against his cap a little longer than necessary. "I agreed to be his campaign manager."

I lifted my face to the ceiling and shook my head with incredulity, mouthing the words, *Oh, my heavenly stars!* Then I lowered my head and said aloud, "Then you've *both* completely lost your minds!"

— ꙮ —

"Listen, James, Alex may be too nice to say anything, but I'm not!" I said about ten or fifteen minutes later after barging into James's house without knocking. "I think you need to know that if you run for president of Fairport, you might as well just stroll down the hall with a bull's-eye attached to your back."

James, who was carefully setting the chess pieces on the board, didn't look up. "I take it you don't think my running for president of the school is a good idea."

"Noooo." I half-laughed. "I'm sorry but I really *don't* think it's a good idea and here's why: You have no chance whatsoever of winning."

"I think I have some pretty good ideas for Fairport," James said to the chessboard.

"He sure does," seconded my brother, his voice vibrating with enthusiasm. "James has come up with some *great* ideas for our school."

"James, please listen to reason." I pulled up a folding chair. "You may have some extraordinary ideas for Fairport. You may have the most wonderful ideas in the world for our school. In fact, I'm sure you even have some really noble hopes and wishes! But you still don't have a chance!" Alex's eyes pierced me with a laser stare. "Well, someone needs to tell him," I said to my brother.

James began tapping one of the pawns on the edge of the table. "I realize there's a good possibility I won't win, but I thought getting some of these ideas out there might help the students— might give them something to think about. Maybe even inspire them."

A good possibility? I shook my head. "Let me try to explain." I pulled my chair even closer and leaned forward, my back straight. "You're dealing with individuals who *don't care,* James." I was speaking slowly in the hopes that James would finally understand the seriousness of the situation. "They don't care about noble causes. They don't care about being better people. They don't care about making Fairport a better school."

James looked up. "Do you really believe that? Because I don't. I give the students of Fairport much more credit than that." James lifted one of the knights from the board and held it midair as he looked me in the eye. "Our classmates may act as if they don't care, Jana, but I think that in reality they *want* to live good, productive lives and that they *want* to believe in something bigger than themselves. I think they're *aching* for something to hold on to."

"James, stop it." I stood up and pressed my fingers against my temples. "I honestly can't stand to hear any more of this nonsense." I was distraught beyond belief that our good friend wasn't grasping what I was trying to tell him. Why was he not hearing me? He just couldn't do this! I *had* to convince him to drop these ludicrous plans!

James repeated his belief in the students of Fairport High

School. It was almost pitiful the way his eyes lit up with such faith and hope.

"Don't you think this is up to James?" Alex said from the cavity in the couch. "Don't you think this is his decision? It's his life."

"Look, James," I was almost pleading now. "We're your friends. It took us a while to . . . I should say it took *me* a while to fully recognize who you are and well, appreciate you. But Alex and I know you. We know what you're like and who you are and that you're . . . you're—" I wanted to say "a remarkable individual," but that sounded pretty over the top, so I said, "a decent human being," instead. "But there are people in our school who . . ." I didn't know how to complete the thought. "You know Lyla Fannen. You know what she's like. She showed her true colors that last day she ate with us after all. She isn't exactly a fan, James. I just don't want to see you hurt."

James chuckled. "No, Lyla and I don't seem to have the same taste in clothes."

I widened my eyes at my brother until I realized that even Alex probably didn't realize how much Lyla hated us now.

"So do you think Lyla Fannen is planning to run for an office?" asked James.

"No," I said, still looking in Alex's direction. It was clear that James wasn't catching on. "Why should she? Lyla understands that she doesn't need an official office. She has all the clout she needs without the work. She'll help determine who wins, however. Lyla will tap her candidate of choice on the shoulder with her scepter and say, 'You're in!'"

In fact, what I was coming to realize was that once Lyla knew that Alex's best friend James was running, she might make it a point to see to it that one of her troops would be in there to annihilate and humiliate James. Maybe she was making plans right now.

My throat tightened as I remembered something Adriana had told me a few days before that I had pushed into some little nook in my brain cavity. There *was* someone Lyla would be tapping on the shoulder and would use for her purposes. Carson Parker had told some of Adriana's dance company friends that *he* planned to run for president. I'd shrugged it off at the time and had told Adriana that the school couldn't get much worse anyway, but now Carson's running suddenly seemed highly significant.

"Was Carson Parker at that meeting yesterday?" I asked James.

"Carson Parker?"

"You must know who Carson Parker is! He looks a lot like that bad boy in *Pinocchio*, the one who turns into a donkey. Only Carson's a bit better looking." As a matter of fact, Carson had been the school's Flashy Floyd until Lyla latched onto him. Straying then became out of the question.

"You mean the one Lyla eats lunch with now?"

"Yes." Rumor had it they did much more than eat lunch together. I had the feeling by the way Lyla made it a point to glue herself to Carson whenever we came around that Carson was kind of a rebound, just-for-show boyfriend.

"I *did* see him there. He's one of the nine of us running for president."

"That's what I was afraid of. That's exactly what I was afraid of." I took a deep breath, held it in, then blew it out slowly.

"Do you think Carson would do a good job as president of Fairport?" James asked.

"Oh, no, but he'll still undoubtedly win. Carson will run such a nasty campaign that whoever runs against him will be made to look like the class fool. And with Lyla backing him this could end up a pretty nasty business. So do you see now, James, why it would be extremely smart of you to pull out while you still can?" I hoped he was finally getting at least a portion of the picture. With Carson Parker running James was not only looking at a lost cause but at an extremely dangerous course as well.

James sat quietly, fully absorbing, I hoped, what I'd just said. But then he raised his head and pushed up his glasses. "I guess we're just going to have to let the students of Fairport decide," he said, his voice firm. "I'm sorry, Jana, but I have a feeling this is something I'm supposed to do, win or lose. And you never know. Sometimes miracles happen."

Heavenly stars! I looked up at the ceiling, opened my mouth, shut it, and shook my head. It wasn't hard to guess what was happening here. I understood by now how my friend operated. He had *a feeling* this was the right thing to do. James was convinced that this spirit, this Holy Ghost he believed in so fervently, was sending him a message from God.

"James, if you're thinking your imaginary little angel might be sitting on your shoulder again, whispering in your ear, maybe you need to move out of fairy-tale land into the real world," I snapped. "If you're—" I didn't finish because Alex had narrowed his eyes and was tilting his head the way he does when I've gone too far. I quit talking as well because, well, I didn't feel that good *myself* about continuing.

"There's always a chance," Alex hissed, his jaw thrust so far forward he looked like the nutcracker prince we display every Christmas, "that James is right. There's no such thing as a lost cause. You never know."

I couldn't stand it. "You're hallucinating! You're both hallucinating! Well, you know what? I don't care what idiocy you two submerge yourselves in. I came here to play chess." I picked up a pawn and slammed it down on a middle square of the board. "Do whatever absolutely ridiculous and moronic things you want to do, just please don't, and I repeat *don't,* involve me!"

Chapter Twelve

For someone who did *not* plan to be involved in my friend's election plans, and who did *not* care, I got very little sleep those next two nights. I kept thinking about poor James and the terrible position he was throwing himself into. I worried about Alex as well. It struck me as tragic that someone who at one time had been a shoo-in for president of Fairport was now the captain of a lost cause. Oh, how I wished I could protect those two from the bludgeoning that I felt was sure to come!

On Monday for approximately a second and a half, I thought things might actually be looking better for James. Adriana met me at my locker with what sounded like great news. "Carson Parker's not running," she said. "He didn't have the grade point." Before I had a chance to express my complete lack of dismay at this development, Adriana finished the story: "Lyla's running now."

As I widened my eyes, Adriana looked around to make sure no one had seen her relay the information. "Oh, boy," I said, my mouth remaining open. "Oh, boy!" I tapped the door of my locker with my fist, then pressed my forehead against it.

This was not only completely and thoroughly unexpected but oh-so not good. I pulled away, took a deep breath, and studied the industrial floor tiles and dull walls that were so unlike the posh pleasant halls of the private school where Mom had wanted us to go. Then I looked back at my friend. "Okay, thanks, Adriana. I'll get the message to James and Alex."

— ∞ —

"Now there is no doubt whatsoever that you will need to talk James into backing out," I almost shouted to my brother a few minutes later from my cell phone in Uncle Bartho's old BMW. I'd begged Mom not to trade in the car because driving it made me feel close to our uncle.

"I'll tell him," Alex said, "but I'll betcha it won't change anything."

He was right, and we both knew it.

After I'd hung up, I just sat there in the school parking lot watching students swarming to their vehicles. I gained consciousness, however, when I noticed Lyla and Carson a few spaces down, laughing at Angela Corbotta who seemed to be having some difficulty getting into her small Focus. Next to James's friend Cassie, Angela was the largest girl in the school.

Lyla spotted me, lifted her hand, and waved at me with delicate fingers, smiling sarcastically. I quickly started the car, jerked it into gear, then slammed on my brakes as I realized I was about to hit a truck that didn't look like it needed any more damage done to it. "My fault. Sorry," I called out to the driver, a boy with acne, braces, and bad hair.

"Hey, Jana, be careful! You might kill off one of Wickenbee's three votes," Carson called. Lyla laughed happily and leaned into him as I quickly rolled up the car window.

— ∞ —

That night I slept even more fitfully than I had the nights before. I dreamed that I was part of a group of people partying on the top floor of a tall building. Alex and James and others were walking along a path far below. The building turned into a school—my school. Dressed in well-made, designer clothing, Lyla and Carson spotted those below and began shouting insults at them. Angela Corbotta was on the path below and so was the boy with bad hair I'd almost run into earlier that day. But then they began aiming their insults at James and Alex. I leaned out a high window and called down to the two tiny dots on the path. "For heaven's sake, you'd better come up here where you belong and hurry!"

Lyla pulled me away from the window. "We don't want them up here," she said.

"It's my brother and our friend," I explained. "They need to enter our building and be a part of things here."

"We don't want *you* here either," Lyla sneered.

In the next frame of my dream I was walking with James and Alex down below on the pavement in front of the building. We were all wearing pants that were too short and multi-colored western shirts with sleeves that didn't come anywhere near our wrist bones and monstrously hideous glasses.

"Look at her!" someone from the building shouted, pointing at *me.* Several more people laughed. Strangely, I didn't seem to mind and instead felt relieved the focus was no longer on Alex and James. In fact, when Lyla and Carson and the others shifted their attention back to James and Alex and started taunting them again, I charged up the building after them, but James reached out to stop me.

"They can't get away with that," I raged.

"Look at the loser!" the people in the building yelled. "Hey, James Orville! Been to church lately, Wickenbee? Hey, Friar James!"

"Just ignore them," Alex said. But I didn't.

"You can't talk to my friend like that!" I started climbing the building like Spiderman. But the group had grown to hundreds of people and all of them had the same fox-red hair as Lyla Fannen. They shouted insults right back until they were all shouting in unison.

Then the building turned into the bleachers of a huge stadium. Alex, James, and I were on the football field, which had acquired squares until it looked like a giant chessboard. Thousands of people in the stands were booing at us and shouting "Losers! Losers!" as if we were the players of the opposing team! When they started throwing things at us, I felt even worse, like a referee. "Push 'em back! Push 'em back! Waaaay back! Losers! Losers! Back! Back!" A tortilla slapped me across the side of my face. More tortillas pelted me, pelted us all, along with empty beer and soda cans, and then potatoes started coming down. I turned and jumped from one square to another to avoid getting hit.

Then suddenly I was hungry and poor again. I began picking up the tortillas and potatoes and stuffing them into my pockets. Lyla was laughing and typing words on a laptop. The words scrolled across the scoreboard in ten-foot high red letters: *Jana Bennings is the biggest loser of all!* The words turned into pictures and then a scene unfolded showing me as I looked in eighth grade in that filthy motel lobby, begging the manager for a few more days of credit. I broke out in a cold sweat.

"Wake up, Sweetheart." Mom was pushing on my back gently. "Jana, you need to get ready. Alex left for jazz band practice almost twenty minutes ago."

Jerking awake, I felt great relief as I realized I was not on a football field but in my own bed and that nobody was throwing anything at me, and that best of all, no scoreboard was revealing any of the more private moments of my life. "Why are you dressed up this early?" I asked my mother.

"Mary Jane and some of the ladies from her church need to get all the toys and quilts for the orphans in Kenya ready today to send to the Salt Lake headquarters. I offered to help. I told you about that, didn't I?"

"I think so." Mom *had* mentioned a service project several days before with what I called the Relief Sisters of the Mormon Church. I didn't need my contacts in to see she'd apparently decided the event called for her nice gray tweed pants and her royal blue silk blouse. She smelled good too—a combination of vanilla lotion and rose bath powder.

Smelling the sweet smell that represented my mother would normally have comforted me, but it didn't help me on this morning. "I don't feel very well," I moaned. "I have a terrible headache." It was oh-so true. My head felt like a giant piñata.

"Do you need to stay home from school?"

"School?" I tried to sit up. "I thought it was Saturday or Sunday."

"It's Tuesday." Mom chuckled quietly. "I told you that Alex left for jazz band practice, remember?" She cocked her head. "You really didn't know it was the middle of the week?"

"Ooooh," I groaned. "Is it really Tuesday? Why couldn't it be *Saturday?*"

Mom frowned. "I'll bring you a glass of water," she offered and left the room.

I pressed the back of my head into my goose-down pillow but then sat up. I tend to get confused and nauseated when I'm overly tired and if this was a school day then I needed to force my limbs to move and my muscles to cooperate. What classes did I have?

I made an attempt to mentally go through my schedule but couldn't seem to find my way past first period French. Why wasn't my brain functioning? At last I was able to emerge from the cotton balls stuffing my brain. *Second period: A.P. English.* English was fine. *Third: A.P. American History.* We'd just had the unit test, and I was well ahead of schedule on my research paper. *Art—no problem. A.P. Physics: again ahead of schedule. Business management?* I could catch up on what I missed. *A.P. Psych: Not good . . .* We were working on a supposed *group* project, which, of course, meant that *I* was single-handedly preparing it. Well, maybe just for today the other group members could get a taste of life without Jana Bennings. Maybe they could even do some of the work for a change. I thought harder. I came to the conclusion that I could miss school this one day without jeopardizing my grades.

Mom came back with a glass of ice water in one hand and a worried expression on her face. She felt my head and checked my pulse. "At least you don't seem to have a fever. But maybe we should take your temperature just to make sure."

"I'm sure I don't have a temperature. I'm just suffering from sleep deprivation."

"I'm not surprised. You work far too hard. I know you like to do well in your classes, but four accelerated courses is just too heavy a load even for someone as intelligent as you are."

I swallowed the water quickly, glad I'd chosen not to tell Mom quite yet that I'd already approached Adriana's father about doing some part-time bookkeeping for his financial planning firm. I was hoping to become a little more knowledgeable about money and earn a few extra dollars, but I knew what my mother would say about it. "We have plenty of money, thanks to your uncle," was her theme song. But we'd found out the hard way *plenty* could disappear overnight. I'd been nervous when Mom had switched from full-time to part-time, working only a couple of days a week. To my relief, she'd picked up some editing assignments on the side and ended up making decent enough money, but I still didn't want to take any chances. Mom and her sisters were completely right-brained when it came to finances and not one of them thought things through clearly or pragmatically when it came to that area.

My mother walked over to my jewelry box and pulled out the pearl earrings I had borrowed for Cotillion two summers before. "You have put too much on your plate. Thank goodness you didn't continue with debate this year." Mom held one of the earrings to her ear then put it back. When she saw my hair pick, she touched up a few areas of her hair. She was, and still is, as particular about her appearance as I am about mine.

"Maybe I *will* stay home today," I said.

Mom carefully replaced the pick in the mother-of-pearl jewelry box then came to the edge of my bed to feel my head again. "That might be a good idea. One of the ladies in Mary Jane's Relief Society, Alona, I think her name was, said both her daughters got mononucleosis their junior year. She said they were the over-achiever types like you. Hopefully you're not already ill. I'll have my cell phone with me if you need anything."

"I'll be fine. I think I'll just try to get some sleep."

"Okay, Sweetheart." Mom smoothed out the far too expensive Laura Ashley bedspread she'd insisted on getting me for my birthday, stroked my hair, handed me an extra pillow, kissed me on the forehead, and then left the room.

I'm not sure how long I stared at the ceiling after my mother left, but finally I opened the blinds and looked out into the backyard. A stray cat was up at the top of our apple tree and seemed to be wondering what he was doing up there. I closed the blinds, plopped back onto my bed, pulled my satin-covered pillow up over my face, and finally got a few hours of much-needed rest.

When I regained consciousness, it was well past lunchtime so I slipped on my terry-cloth bathrobe and my Mickey Mouse slippers and flopped down the stairs. When I got to the kitchen, I prepared myself a bowl of Raisin Bran. Carrying the bowl with me, I wandered into the alcove near the stairs where we keep a small table for magazines such as *Time, Newsweek, Sports Illustrated,* and *House and Garden.* I'd read them all already, but there was a fairly old copy of *Woman's Day,* a makeover edition, under some newspapers.

I like before and after pictures so I flipped through a few pages. Most of the women looked better in the after pictures, but a few didn't. A twenty-five-year-old sales rep now looked like a sex rep with all that makeup. The "experts" had gone way too skimpy on the clothing. What? Had they run out of fabric? *No, Alicia,* I thought to the woman in the picture, *you looked far better before.* But an older woman, Beverly, had started off with rather long stringy hair and looked much better with her chic new cut and style. I did think she needed to rethink the ultra short leather miniskirt, however.

I thumbed through a few more pages and stopped at an article entitled, "The Superman Chronicles," which reviewed the lives of the actors who had played Superman, including my favorite, Christopher Reeve. It still seemed to me a cruel twist of fate that this actor who'd made the perfect Superman had taken a fall that had paralyzed him and eventually taken his life. I'd even liked Christopher Reeve as Clark Kent.

I shut the magazine, but a few seconds later I opened it again and stared at the picture of a young, handsome, and virile Reeve in his Superman getup. I tapped my nails against my empty cereal bowl. Slowly I lifted myself out of the chair.

We have a fairly good-sized entertainment and recreation room downstairs and I made my way down there. I sifted through the stack of movies on the TV, then thumbed through the videos in the large built-in maple case. Even though we preferred DVDs, Alex still had quite a few movies on videotape. If Alex put it back, *Superman* would be on the vintage action movie shelf. My fingers danced over the spines: the *Batman* movies, *Rambo* one and two, *Rocky*—one through twenty-nine—and the *Star Wars* series. Sure enough, there it was.

Holding the cereal spoon in my mouth, I turned on the VCR, slipped the movie into the slot, and fast-forwarded to where I thought the scene I was looking for would be. There it was! The scene where Christopher Reeve, alias Clark Kent, smiles, lifts his body, and removes his glasses. Just like that, without even switching into his costume, he's transformed into Superman. I played the scene again and again. We really needed to get this on DVD!

Back upstairs, I headed to the drawer of our rosewood cabinet where I was pretty sure I'd abandoned my old glasses after I'd gotten contacts. That's exactly where I found the beasts. With a grimace of disgust, I put them on and walked into the family room to the mirror over the fireplace.

Ever since finishing school I've had excellent posture, but now I slumped forward and pulled my glasses halfway down the bridge of my nose. Because I had to look up over the rim of my glasses, I lowered my head as well and stood like that for several seconds. I turned sideways, then forward again, took my glasses off, and lifted myself to my full height. Even in my bathrobe and my hair a mess, the contrast was astounding. *Okay, one more time.*

Laughing a little, I donned the glasses and slumped once more, then pulled myself up again, taking off the glasses just like Clark Kent had. The difference that such a small change could make really was intriguing. I stood there staring into the mirror at myself as Super-Jana. Then I raised an eyebrow. A smile began to form.

Chapter Thirteen

I have a plan!" I said excitedly to James and Alex. I'd called Alex the second I knew school was over to arrange a meeting with them at James's house.

"Have a nice day off, Ferris?" Alex asked as soon as I arrived at James's.

I ignored the statement and reference to one of his all-time favorite old movies and didn't so much as flicker an eyelash. There was no time for small talk or bantering! "Here's what I'm thinking. Picture a huge banner with a *before* picture of you, James, on one end. The banner reads: 'Watch James Wickenbee turn into Super-Jim!'"

"A *before* picture?" James looked confused. "Before what?"

"Let me rephrase that. On one end we place a large picture of what you look like now. But on the other end, we leave a blank square for another picture of you. Under it we write, 'Fairport's Next President.' As the campaign progresses, James, you improve—

and again, let me rephrase that—your appearance improves. A day or two before the election we place a picture of the new and improved you in that spot—your new picture, the *after* picture— which shows you as Super-Jim. We can even follow this Superman or Super-Jim theme throughout our campaign. Our committee members can wear T-shirts with a big letter 'S' on them, and we'll hand out fliers with the Superman emblem on them that say 'Vote for Super-Jim!'"

James still looked confused. "I'm really happy you've decided to help us, Jana, but I'm not sure I understand what you mean when you say that my appearance will improve."

"It won't happen all at once." My voice was uneven and all my words came out in a rush. I couldn't believe how excited I was about this! It was obvious, though, I needed to transfer some of that excitement to James and Alex—especially James. After all, he was the one who would be doing the changing and so far he wasn't acting particularly caught up in my plan.

"You've seen those talk shows where they bring out someone and show that person before, and then they send that person to some professional hairstylists, fashion experts, and so forth, and he or she comes out looking like a new person?" I continued, still talking fast.

"I don't watch TV much, but I take it you mean where they do an overhaul on somebody's appearance?"

"Exactly. It's called a makeover."

"That's right. Uh-huh." He rubbed his forehead. "No offense, Jana, but I'm really not into that type of thing."

"Do you have a full-length mirror anywhere?"

"Probably somewhere. There could be one in the basement." I wasn't surprised that James didn't know where the family's full-length mirror was. "But like I say—"

"It's in our room—the master bedroom." James's mother had poked her head into the living room and was smiling broadly. "On the back of the closet door."

"Thank you." I smiled only slightly in return and raised my eyebrows a little at her. Mary Jane took the hint and disappeared back into the kitchen. In a lower voice, I listed a few more things that I'd need in order to give James a better idea of what I was talking about. He reluctantly left the room with his assignment.

"Take it easy on him," Alex whispered. "Try to be subtle."

"I'm always subtle."

"Right . . . uh-huh." Alex lifted his eyes toward the ceiling.

After a few minutes James came back into the room juggling the mirror under his arm, a plastic spray bottle of water, and a brush and comb. He leaned the mirror against the bookcase and pulled up a chair. "I'm not sure why I'm doing this, but—"

"Just trust me. Okay, let's see." While I ran my fingers through his hair, he nervously pushed up his glasses. "Now your hair's not a bad texture, and it's a good rich brown, but this style's not right for you. We'll need to get you some help there."

"What do you mean by *style?* I've always worn it this way."

"Here, I'll show you." I sprayed his hair until it was fairly wet. "Wearing your hair straight back does nothing at all for you."

I'd accidentally sprayed his glasses and James pulled a tissue from a box next to an old console and wiped them dry without taking them off.

I parted his hair and combed it forward. "When this dries, you'll see how much better this looks on you. Of course, you'll need a good hairstylist to cut it for you before it'll really look like it should. I'll make an appointment for you with Raphael. He's expensive but worth it. Next—posture. Stand up please."

James rose slowly, apprehensively.

I nudged him sideways. "Okay, now take a good look."

"I always remind him to stand up straight," offered Mary Jane, who had appeared this time through the opening between the kitchen and living room.

I immediately stopped talking and with a slow, exaggerated turn in her direction stared at her with my head lowered.

"I tell all my children that," she said with much less confidence. "But you kids go ahead. I won't interfere anymore." She backed away quickly from the opening, and I heard her muttering something about going down to her lab. It was for the best. This wasn't something a mother should see.

"Okay," I said, lowering my voice again. "Let's continue. Here's the thing, James. People can't see themselves in action. If we all had cameras following us around, we'd know what we looked like and we'd probably be astounded, but we don't. How you stand is vitally important. Alex, can you pull back James's shoulders?"

After Alex had forced himself out of the comfortable corduroy chair, he placed both hands on James's shoulders and tugged. At precisely the same time I pressed the back of my hand hard against the small of James's back.

"Aaargh! Hey!" James thrust out the upper front portion of his body.

95

"Ah-ha, I knew you had a chest in there! So far, so good."

"Look, I'm not . . . This is . . ." He pushed at his glasses.

"Now this is the important part, James," I continued, ignoring his attempts at complaint. "Pretend you're being pulled skyward— or in your case, we'll call it *heavenward.*"

"Heavenward, huh?" James blew out air and shook his head. As he lifted himself straight, he immediately locked his knees, a common mistake.

"Don't go swayback on us," I said.

In my ninth-grade PE class, Mrs. Creel had had us all flatten our backs against the gymnasium wall. That was the first time I'd realized that in order to get the small of the back lined up, it was necessary to bend the knees slightly. That fact was confirmed in my finishing course. Boys and men don't take finishing courses, and I doubted that male gym coaches discussed posture in boy's PE.

"Bend your knees slightly," I said. "Okay . . there you go." I lifted his chin. "That's so much better." I stepped back, nodding with some measure of satisfaction.

"Dude, I think you just grew five inches," Alex said, amazed. "Coach Rigby will be after you to play basketball."

Mary Jane peeked around the side of the opening again. When I turned in her direction, she jerked back and disappeared as quickly as she'd appeared. "I'm heading to the lab right now," she said. "I'm on my way."

"Seriously . . ." Alex couldn't get over the transformation. "I've heard of growth spurts but, not half a foot in thirty seconds."

There was much more to do and I was anxious to move on. "Now, about your clothes, James—"

"What's wrong with my clothes?"

"What's *not* wrong with them? No more wearing Fred's or worse, *Felix's,* shirts and pants!"

"Hey, as long as my brothers aren't here to wear their clothes, why shouldn't I go ahead and . . ." James's voice trailed off because I'd adjusted the mirror so that he could see that his pants, undoubtedly Felix's, ended several inches above his ankles.

"Unless you're going for the Capri look," I drawled.

James continued staring at his thick white socks which were extremely noticeable because they were extremely exposed. "Oh." He paused. "I didn't realize I'd outgrown these pants."

"I have the feeling there are a lot of things you haven't realized. But don't worry, we'll go through Alex's closet. It looks like you two are both around six feet, give or take a half-inch. Alex bought a couple of shirts the other day in colors that tend to wash him out but they might work for you."

Alex shut one eye and moved back a little.

"Nobody's perfect," I said to my brother. "Not even you, Alex." I turned back to James. "There might be some decent pants for you as well in Alex's closet. We have to begin work on your walk right away."

James sighed, scratched his neck, and mumbled something.

"And the mumbling will need to stop," I continued. "Heavenly stars, there's *so* much, it's overwhelming! Thank goodness your teeth will only need some whitening. Obviously, there's no time for even minor dental work." James pushed up his glasses again. "And oh, yes, those glasses . . ."

James immediately pressed his glasses against the bridge of his nose as though he were trying to permanently attach them there. "My glasses? I like these glasses. What *about* my glasses?"

"I'm guessing you're farsighted. You probably don't even need to wear them all the time."

"It seems like a waste of time to keep taking them off, putting them back on, and finding them in between."

"I know," I said. "I've seen you walk down the halls with them perched on the end of your nose, peering at people over them. That really needs to stop. How you look at people is extremely important. You can't expect to become president of a school by peering at people. And that's another thing. You need to get rid of the scowl."

I knew I was being hard on James, but sometimes you have to hit hard and fast for it to stick. Now that I'd analyzed him more closely, I realized James really did have some decent material to work with, but we had very little time. He needed to cooperate completely if we were going to make this happen.

"What scowl? I don't—" James checked in the mirror again and saw that he was scowling at that very second. "Oh."

"That's right. You peer at people over your ridiculous glasses while you scowl at them. It's a bad habit."

"Tone it down," said Alex, obviously irritated with me. "Why are you repeating yourself?"

"To make my point!" I tried to take James's glasses from him again, but he pressed them back against his nose with even greater force.

"I mean it. Take it easy, Jana," Alex warned.

"Okay!" Since I couldn't very well pry James's glasses out from under his fingers, I lowered my hand and took a couple of steps back. My brother was right about my tendency to become too intense at times. "Okay, okay, you're right. We can't do this all at once. James, we'll leave your glasses alone for now, but we need to really zero in on your posture immediately. Starting tomorrow, we'll have committee members reminding you to stand up straight. A thumbs up means stand up." I lifted my thumb. "This will be our sign to you that you need to straighten your shoulders and your back and imagine strings from heaven pulling you up— all of that.

"That reminds me. That's something else we need to work on right away. We need to get on the phone and get a committee started immediately. Make a list of all the . . . ummm . . . all the people you know who might be willing to help."

I was smart enough to avoid the word "dorks" but knew that the less-than-sought-after students might be the only ones we'd be left with for our committee.

First of all, I doubted that very many of those I considered *normal* classmates would be hopping on this particular bandwagon. Adriana, simply because she was a close friend, would possibly help a little if it wasn't at school or where anyone else would know she was involved. I was sure Michelle Wilcox, as a fellow member of James's church, would have been willing to jump in had she not already agreed to be Ruby Backus's campaign manager. Alex's friends Rob and Pete were already helping Brad Jenkins and his yell-leader friends were backing Lucas Hart. In fact, just about all those I considered the "good people" had been snatched up quickly by the other candidates.

"Sorry about this, James." Alex's eyelids were lowered partway, his eyebrows drawn together. "Jana tends to think she's the queen mother. I've had to deal with it my whole life."

But James was busy studying himself in the mirror. "No . . . no . . . it's okay. In fact, you know what? I think I needed this." He turned so that Alex could get the full picture. James's hair still needed a lot of work, but we could at least get an idea of how it would eventually look. He was standing to his full height and his chest and shoulders looked strong and firm. With the exception of his clothes and glasses, James looked good. He looked, well *almost*, like a Super-Jim. It shut Alex right up.

Chapter Fourteen

W e held our first committee meeting at James's the following day. Derrick Farn turned out to be an ace on the computer and pecked away at the keyboard as if it were chicken feed. I already knew Sadie Rice was painfully shy, but she had more than adequate skills with a yardstick.

"Not bad," I said, when, with a sniff-like snort, she whispered that she'd finished the rough draft of one of the banners.

Mary Jane had found an old picture of James which Bud said he could enlarge at Kinkos where he worked. It was a goofy looking picture and absolutely perfect. Bud volunteered as well to get to school early on Friday and hang the banners up high enough in good spots for everyone to see. At six-foot-seven I knew Bud probably wouldn't need a ladder. He *was* a ladder.

"I'll get Terrance to help me," he said excitedly, licking his lips.

"I'll go too!" Cassie pulled herself up with surprising agility.

"Now remember if anybody sees James slumping anytime,

anywhere, during the day, we give him the thumbs up signal. It won't mean 'good job' this time. It'll mean 'stand up straight!' It's important we all remind James."

"You got it!" Cassie belted out.

"But let's keep it subtle," I added, as I pressed my finger against my ear. I could just picture her shouting at James from miles down the hall, or worse, the whole group of them tailgating him. But then I frowned. Maybe we'd have the opposite problem. There were so few of us that maybe we wouldn't be reminding James often enough. I'd read it takes about three weeks to acquire a new habit, and James had just a day or two before we'd need to move on to the next major change.

"It might not be a bad idea to tie a string around your thumb or wind some tape around your wrist to remind yourself to stand tall," I told him. "Better yet . . ."—and this illustrates pretty well how sensitive and compassionate I was back then—I grabbed the wooden yardstick and broke it in two. "Here, tape this to your back. You can't rely on someone always being there to remind you and this should help."

James stared at the jagged end of the yardstick. "I'll just go with the tape, thanks."

"I don't blame you, Dude," said Alex, looking at me with contempt.

"There's a lot at stake here," I said defensively.

— ∞ —

Things went remarkably well that next day in school. Amazingly, James was walking or standing tall every time I spotted him. I still couldn't get over how much just that one element improved his appearance. Interestingly, as committee members reminded him to watch his posture, they all began standing up straighter as well. I saw Cassie straightening her own back as she lifted her thumb at James during lunch. But when she looked down at her huge body, she slumped again and pulled three or four granola bars out of her pocket.

We'd been working on James's posture only a couple of days when I overheard Maisie Cox, whose locker was near mine, say to Melissa Fairchild, "You know that James Wickenbird or Wickenbacher or whatever his name is—the guy with the strange glasses who's running for president? Was he always that tall? I wonder if he had back surgery or something. My cousin was three inches taller after she had surgery for scoliosis. She went from five-four to five-seven."

"He's just standing up straighter," I heard myself say to the girls. "Haven't you noticed his banners?"

Maisie swung around, flinching and scrunching her nose—an unattractive habit. "Oh, hi, Jana! What banners?"

"They're all over. You might want to look for James's banners and tell your friends to look for them. It's a clever theme." I was talking fast. "It says 'Watch James turn into Super-Jim.' We're offering rewards to people who figure out each day what's improved about James." I flinched and scrunched my nose a little myself at this admission of being involved.

"Fun!" Maisie responded. "I love makeovers! So will he get better clothes too?"

"That's definitely in the plans."

"Good. His clothes are kind of—"

"Hideous?"

"Well, yes. And they sometimes seem too small for him. His shirts anyway."

She was right. James had become quite conscientious about wearing longer pants, but he still apparently grabbed one of Felix's shirts out of the closet once in a while. "You're very observant, Maisie. In fact, we could use someone like you on our committee."

"Really? Who else is on it?"

"Alex and me and . . . quite a few others," I said evasively. *Never mind,* I thought. "Hey, listen, while you're deciding, here are a few fliers you could hand out. Would you mind?"

"Okay, sure . . . sure . . ." She stared down at the fairly substantial stack. "I guess I could do that."

I smiled at her and headed for class before she could change her mind.

— ∞ —

After school that day Alex and I went through his closet and pulled out some stylish shirts and pants in colors that would look good with James's dark hair. Even in jeans a person needs to look put together.

"Let's run over to his house right now," I said eagerly. "I'm anxious that he try these on."

"We're not playing Barbie, you know," Alex said.

"I know," I said. *"Ken."*

A little while later, as James surveyed himself in the stylish-but-casual blue shirt and Alex's designer cargo pants from last year, he looked extremely pleased with himself. "I think these are the nicest clothes I've ever worn. Thanks for letting me borrow them." He took a couple of steps back, and I could tell he was checking to see whether the pants were long enough.

"The pants are exactly the right length," I assured him.

He seemed to agree and maybe would have let his new look go to his head if I hadn't pressed the heel of my hand into the small of his back. He was slumping again. James lurched forward.

"Warn the guy," said Alex.

"That *would* be nice," said James, grimacing.

"Aw, but then it wouldn't be nearly as effective, would it?" I stood in front of James and placed my hands on his shoulders. "Look, James, you can wear all the brand names and classiest clothes in the world and they won't look good on you if you slump and lean forward like that. I have to say that you've been doing remarkably well, but we don't have time for you to let up for even a few minutes."

With a puff of impatience, James once again pulled back his shoulders. Then he remembered the make-believe heavenly strings and lifted his upper body as well.

"Your knees," I reminded him. "You're locking your knees."

"That's right, the knees," he said without inflection.

This time I sighed. "I knew this would be hard," I complained to Alex, who was eating one of the ham sandwiches Mary Jane had left out for us, "but I had no idea *how* difficult."

"It's hard for *you*?" Alex said facetiously as he flecked some mustard from the corner of his mouth with the side of his thumb and rubbed it into his napkin. "What about me? I'm feeling the pressure all the time to come up with the cute outfits."

Alex got the reaction he was looking for. "Oh, yes, very funny, poor you!" The sandwich looked good and I asked him for a bite.

"Get your own."

"But I don't want a whole one."

"You always say that and then you eat most of mine."

James pulled a plastic knife from a pencil holder, rinsed it off, and cut off a section of the sandwich still remaining. "Here," he said.

"Oh, thanks." I took a careful bite as I continued arguing with my brother about which of us had done the most work and which of us was suffering the most from all of this work with James.

James moved quietly to the couch. He seemed to be thinking and worrying. When I gave him the thumbs up, he didn't move, and I had to lift my thumb again. "Yoo-hoo, James."

"Right. Okay." James tried to sit up straighter, which wasn't easy to do from a sofa sinkhole.

"All right, Alex," I said, looking for a napkin. "You win. Your life is really tough. But this isn't about you or me. It's about James! So let's get back to work!" I'd found the napkins and wiped off my mouth, then looked through my bag for my checklist. "Hmmm, let's see now . . ." I scrutinized my notes. "It looks like you have an appointment tomorrow at noon with Raphael, James. Better write that down."

"Who?"

"My hairstylist. I'll get you the address. I'll call ahead to make sure he understands what we want—maybe I'd better even go along." Yes, I'd go along! I couldn't expect James to give Raphael detailed instructions. "Now walking lessons are at two and chess is at three."

"We're still playing chess?" James sounded highly relieved that we'd be stopping for some R and R.

"Of *course* we're still playing chess." I was relieved myself that there was something to look forward to besides work, work, and more work! In any event, our chess game had become an established ritual; skipping it was unthinkable. I needed that weekly game. Spending time at the Wickenbees' each Saturday from three to five or five-thirty gave me a feeling of peace, stability, and security that revitalized me for the week. I wasn't sure I could function without it anymore.

"Hey, I have a question, Jana," Alex said, as he finished off the last bite of ham. "When did *you* become James's campaign manager? I thought *I* was the campaign manager." My brother was somewhat kidding, but not completely. "Once again you've taken over. You tend to do that."

"Fine, *you* call Raphael and instruct him on how to cut James's hair," I countered. "Raphael has a very creative side and I don't want James showing up at school with purple streaks and a bouffant. Tell Raphael to stick to a good basic look—classic men's haircut, no line—then watch him like a hawk. And be sure you pronounce his name correctly: Rrrrr-aphael—with a roll on the *r*. He comes unglued if you mispronounce it."

"I delegate dealing with Rrrrr-aphael to you," said Alex quickly. He turned to James. "But if Miss Control Freak here will allow us

107

to squeeze it into your busy schedule, we should go lift weights at the gym sometime tomorrow. You and me, man."

Having James buff up was an excellent idea. In fact, I was surprised I hadn't thought of it. James had nice wide shoulders, but his arms were undefined and even a little skinny. "That's not a bad idea, Alex," I admitted. The prospect of a toned-up and in shape Super-Jim excited me. "Just don't get carried away. We don't want him looking like one of those muscle-bound, no-neck, Arnold types. I hate that look."

Alex laughed. "As if. You don't turn into an Arnold in days or even weeks. There's no way we're going to see six-pack abs. But I *do* think we could see some pretty good results in the upper arms and shoulders."

"I'll tell you what, we'll postpone walking lessons. Just get James back in time for our chess game."

Alex saluted.

Chapter Fifteen

T he following Monday, Emily Fitzmeier, a girl in my physics
class rushed up to me. "His hair!" she exclaimed.

"What?"

"I heard we get a prize if we guess what's changed about James
Wicken—something—and it's his hair!"

I was ecstatic that word seemed to be getting around. "Good
job! Here!" I handed her about two dozen red-white-and-blue
S fliers.

"This is my prize?"

"For the moment." I hadn't actually thought up the prizes yet.
"And here comes our hero now!" I said.

Emily jerked around and smiled widely as the main attraction,
namely James, came ambling down the hall. Several other students
were staring at him.

"You're looking pretty good," I told him quietly, "except that
you're leaning forward a little."

James nodded and pulled his shoulders farther back.

"She needs a whip, doesn't she, James?" said Alex, who was just coming out of history class.

"How would you like to be on James's committee?" I asked Emily, who was now standing between James and Alex, happily gazing up from the much-improved-in-the-eye-appeal-department, dark-haired James to my handsome, pale-haired brother.

"Sure," said Emily. "I'd like that."

"Why *Emily* . . ." I recognized the silky voice immediately and I turned slowly. "You're on *my* committee, remember?" Alex hadn't mentioned Lyla was in his history class—I'd have been a little more cautious if he had—but sure enough, there she was, standing in Mr. Stewart's doorway, smiling with fake sweetness and looking stunning even in distressed Levis.

"Oh, that's right." Emily blinked hard. "I forgot. I'm with Lyla."

Lyla wrinkled her nose at us, smiled, and took Emily by the arm. "I don't think Emily here really fits in anyway with your umm . . . shall we say . . . *unusual* group?"

I winced inwardly, opened my mouth, but then shut it.

"Unusual" was, unfortunately, still a completely accurate description of our committee. We had ten people on it now and more joining all the time but so far there wasn't a *usual* person in the bunch. With the exception of Adriana, who stopped by once in a while out of pure loyalty to me and Alex, these were the students at Fairport who had probably not had much chance to be on committees of any kind. These were the people who had probably never been invited to be in much of anything. I pictured them being picked last for sports and activities all through elementary and junior high school. I pictured them being left out of the games at recess.

"I guess we should feel fortunate we even *have* committee members," I admitted quietly to Alex as the girls walked away.

"*Enthusiastic* committee members!" Alex reminded me. It was an adjective that once again I had to admit really did apply. Maybe our committee members weren't the "in" people of the school, and maybe as I suspected, they had never *been* "in" people, but nobody could call them shirkers. They worked with intense, pure, and raw *enthusiasm*.

When Sadie got excited, however, it seemed to make her sinus problems worse. She would make three or four small snorts in a row, wheeze, then snort several more times. As voting day got closer, Derrick pecked into the air more rapidly, his hair bouncing up and down. Cassie seemed to eat more when she got excited and Brother Bud, as James called him, less. Cassie had also been shouting out "Wowsers!" far too loudly and too often and greeting everyone, including me, with huge, lung-collapsing hugs.

"Cassie," I said at lunch, gasping for breath, "I thought we talked about that."

"I know, I know."

But how could any of us really complain too much about Cassie's exuberance when she'd put that same kind of energy into her campaign work? In fact, all the committee members were working tirelessly. Our committee had increased to even more relentless workers, and James was getting reminded every few minutes to stand up straight, watch his walk, and speak clearly. The Super-Jim crew seemed to be everywhere.

— ᴼᴼᵟ —

"Maybe we need to back off poor James just a little," Alex said on Tuesday before the primary elections. "Can't we give the guy a rest?"

"Of course we can't," I answered. "We have only hours left."

At our meeting that night, four-and-a-half-foot tall Garlia Ponovich, our newest committee member and a little rougher type than the rest, asked, "So when do the freakin' glasses go?" She pulled out a cigarette, then remembering we'd told her no smoking, pushed it back into the package, mumbling under her breath.

Cigarettes were just one of the "freakin'" things Garlia herself needed to get rid of. She boasted twenty-three piercings: two in each eyebrow, three on her bottom lip, six in each ear, and the three in her nose. I suspected from the garbled way she spoke that her tongue was piercing number twenty-three.

"Yes, everybody's wondering that. When will his glasses go?" Breathing heavily, Cassie pushed her own glasses toward the bridge of her nose. They slid right back down. Cassie's nose was the only part of her that wasn't fat. It was a long aristocratic even enviable nose.

"Patience," I said. "His glasses come off last. That'll be the grand finale."

"I totally can't wait! Wowser—" Cassie slapped her hand over her mouth. "Sorry."

That night when I thought Alex was finally doing his calculus homework, I suddenly realized he was staring at me instead.

"What?"

"You've surprised me this last week or two," he said.

"Why's that?"

"I thought social standing meant everything to you and that you only wanted to associate with people on the Fairport social register."

"I was making those connections for *you*, Alex. Believe me it was painful." My statement wasn't entirely true. Although I had not enjoyed the company of the school's "socially elite" per se, I had to admit, I *had* liked the prestige of being considered one of them. I had enjoyed the status, in other words. "And I'm associating with umm . . . well, those, as you say, who are not on or anywhere near the Fairport social register, only because James is a good friend," I continued in a lower voice. "We couldn't very well let him swim for his life out there all by himself, now could we?"

"No, we couldn't." Alex continued staring at me.

"What? You think I can't tell genuine quality?" I asked. "You think I only look at the superficial?"

"Let's just say I'm happily surprised that you've been willing to risk other things for this cause—like your own image, for instance."

I sighed and nodded. I was pretty sure I knew what he was referring to. Alex had seen me just that day giving Derrick and Sadie some last-minute instructions right in the front hall. Oh, I'd tried to interact with committee members only away from school, but it had proven to be impossible to run a campaign that way. As

Derrick—to my mortification—had pecked his way through the list and Sadie had snorted with ferocity, Katrina Utley, one of Lyla's friends, had rolled her eyes, and whispered something to Scott Wilkes.

Yes, I would have much preferred to have been whispering to gorgeous Scott Wilkes myself, but unfortunately he wasn't on our committee. And no, it wasn't easy for me, but what choice did I have? When a friend finds himself flailing in water over his head, you jump in and help him out. I just hoped we weren't making all this effort only to end up sinking together into some deep abyss.

"I don't know what's going to happen, Alex, but there's no turning back. If we don't continue giving it all our effort these next couple of days and do everything we can to get James elected, I know we'll be sorry. Sure, the chance that there will be a big payoff later is extremely small, but since James refused to back away from this, we really had no choice but to at least try to help him." *And it will all be over soon,* I added to myself.

"I'm with you!" Alex said, flipping out his hand, palm-side up.

I gave him five, and he gave me five right back and then, grinning, almost beaming, my brother did some kind of fancy hand thing. I hesitated but then reciprocated with a hand thing of my own. Shaking my head, I couldn't help smiling at my brother's obnoxious, but naïve exuberance. He could be so juvenile.

"You're definitely a dork," I said, my voice a mixture of disgust and love. "But then," I added, with a half sigh, "aren't we all?"

Chapter Sixteen

To my satisfaction, the makeover project on James had become the talk of the school. On Wednesday I actually overheard a girl in the restroom call James "yummy."

"Well, I mean except for those fake glasses. Are they hysterical, or what?"

"I know. This is almost as good as *Ultimate Makeover*," said her friend who sported a bright yellow crew cut.

When I told James at lunch about the compliments I'd been hearing, he seemed more concerned than excited. "People seem to be paying more attention to what's going on with the way I look than my ideas for the school," he complained.

"That'll come," I said. "We get you the image, then you get listeners. That's how it works."

He sighed, nodded, and pushed back his glasses. James knew I was making sense.

— ᴏᴅ —

That night, James came over for his last makeover session. Amazingly, his biceps had filled out in just those few days. He was also looking really good in Alex's jeans and a blue T-shirt.

"I got you new glasses," I said, removing his baseball cap so it didn't push down his ears.

"I think mine are fine," said James.

"No, James, they're really not." I held out my hand. "I promise I'll keep them in a safe place for you."

James did not hand over his glasses.

"Please, James. We both know you can't keep wearing those and expect to win this election."

Again, James pushed his glasses tighter against the bridge of his nose. "I like these old glasses. Okay, they may not be the latest style, but I've worn them since seventh grade."

"I can tell," I said, "but I have a gift for you." I pulled a slim glasses case from my bag and slid out the slick new designer frames I'd just picked up at Derricott Optical. "Contacts would be better—that's what Alex and I wear—but it takes time to get used to them. The first week Alex wore his contacts he didn't apply enough moisture or something. One got stuck in his eye and it took him a full hour to pry it out. You can't risk walking around with bloodshot eyes right now. And since you're farsighted, I don't know if contacts would even work anyway. Besides, you won't need to wear glasses all the time. When you don't need them, just slip them into your shirt pocket."

"Maybe I could get a cord or something and just hang my glasses around my neck where they'll be handy," James suggested.

"Yes, and we could also call you Dame Edna." I turned and widened my eyes at Alex, then turned back to James. "No, I don't think so. Let's stick with your shirt pocket." I showed him how quickly he could slip his glasses into his pocket, one ear handle over the pocket edge. "Then, you pull them out, see? *Voila!*" I flipped them open, ready for use. "Details matter, James."

James pushed his old glasses even tighter against his head.

"Under no circumstances are you to peer over these new glasses. This is important. Also, no more shaking hands these last couple of days. We should have discussed this right from the beginning. Shaking hands is fine for your brothers who are missionaries, but you're to give people five. Better yet, point at them."

"Now wait a minute, Mom said pointing is rude," said Alex in a high nasal voice. He grinned and pointed at me. "I remember."

"Not if you point the right way—like this." I demonstrated how I'd seen the football jocks lumber down the hall, stop, lean back, lift their head, extend their index finger at the party they were greeting, then continue. "At least that's how I've seen *you* do it, Alex," I said lifting my eyebrows at my brother, who was pressing his fist over his mouth in an effort not to laugh at my impersonation of a jock. "But let's practice the high fives first," I said, ignoring him.

Sadie, who, it turned out, had some excellent computer skills, was nearby, working away on our agenda for the following day. Other committee members had come as well to watch this final big unveiling. Cassie, who was sharing a sweet roll with Bud, handed him a napkin. They interacted a great deal like Alex and I did.

"Okay, everybody, come join us. Let's all practice the high fives."

Sadie turned away from the computer with a big sniff, stood up slowly and looked toward her cousin Derrick and then at Cassie. "Right here, Sadie," I said, lifting my hand. She gently patted my palm. "Let's try that again with a little more power this time."

Sadie bit down on the tip of her tongue, and slapped my palm with much greater energy.

"Good job!"

Soon all the committee members were giving each other high fives, or at least trying. Most of the time, they connected. Bud thought it was great fun to lift his hand so high that people had to jump to reach him. "You're going to have to stick to low fives," I told him. Then I suggested the committee members stand in a row and let James walk by and give each person a high five and a low five. Gradually the slapping died down. "Okay," I said, turning to James. "The time has come. We're all here to back you up, but it's time to turn in your glasses." I reached for James's glasses once again.

"Maybe later."

"James, there is no later. You've got to do this," I said with exasperation. "Come on, you're being stubborn!"

James sighed deeply. "Okay, okay. You're right. Just give me a few seconds." James took a deep breath, slowly lifted his glasses from his nose, and stared at them. Sadie put her hand over her mouth, Cassie applauded softly, and Adriana stretched her lips at me in amazement.

James walked over to the desk drawer and pulled out an old brown glasses case. He pushed the glasses carefully inside, tucked it closed, placed the case in the drawer, and pushed the drawer shut. After he'd studied the new glasses, he slid them onto his nose and pushed them against his forehead. It was a symbolic moment.

"Now," I said, "come take a look in the mirror."

James followed me to the mirror, where he studied himself intently. He moved closer to the mirror and then backed up a little. "These aren't all that bad. I can see pretty well through them."

"That's not surprising since I got the prescription from your mother. But let's talk about the important part: How do you look in them?"

Adriana was happy to give her opinion. "I really like his eyes in them," she said. "You look great, James."

"Thanks, Adriana," James said with surprising poise considering he'd probably never received a compliment from anyone as decent-looking as Adriana before.

"Okay, James, now let's practice having you slip these new glasses into your shirt pocket," I said.

James did as he was told and did a good job. "Okay everyone! Meet Super-Jim." I turned James around. "What do you think, folks?"

Sadie moved her hair out of her eyes. "You look . . . uhhh . . . *super*." She snorted, then giggled.

"Wowsers!" screeched Cassie. "WOW—SERS!" She began doing a jig then, portions of her body shifting from side to side. I honestly didn't mind hearing her shouts of enthusiasm that day. They were echoing my own sentiments!

"Alex, can you find that old instant camera? I still haven't been able to get our new digital to work—something's wrong with it—and we need a picture right this second of our creation."

"I brought my digital camera," Terrance said shyly.

"Good job, Terrance!" I was impressed. "We need to enlarge this next picture for our banner by tonight. Tomorrow, James, you're Super-Jim. On second thought, let's not have you wear glasses at all for the final photo."

Terrance lifted his camera and pressed a button to zoom in on James's face.

"Wait a sec," I said. James's hair was pressed down too tightly and needed just a little help before Terrance snapped the photo. As I fluffed James's hair with my fingers, I happened to glance into James's eyes. The sunlight from the window across the room was reflecting in them and I gasped. When he wore his glasses, especially the old ones, you hardly noticed his eyes. Now I could see that James had the clearest, bluest eyes imaginable. "My stars, Adriana, you're right."

"What?" asked James with concern. "So now what's wrong?"

"Nothing's wrong. Something's very right. I just noticed that you have incredible eyes! In fact, Terrance, let's snap the picture from this angle. Right now." I couldn't believe I'd never noticed this amazing asset before. It was like finding a diamond in sandstone. "James, your eyes are . . . Here, everybody look at James's eyes!"

Sadie came up close, unusually close for her, I thought, until I remembered that she too was farsighted and had broken her own glasses a few days before. Not that you ever saw her glasses with the way her hair always covered her face. Now she pushed some wisps away from her eyes. "Wowsers!" She jerked back, lowered her head in surprise at herself, drew in her breath, but then couldn't help herself and moved closer again.

Wowsers? Now Sadie was saying it.

"Double, no, *triple* wowsers!" added Cassie, equally enthralled.

"Are they great eyes or what?" I said.

"You just might win this thing," garbled Garlie.

"Because of my eyes?" Once again I could tell this bothered James. "I'd rather people listened to my ideas. But I guess this will all be over soon."

"The eyes are conduits of the soul," I proclaimed, unsure whether I was making that up or if I'd read it somewhere.

"That is a nice thought, Jana." James smiled at me then—a from the heart, appreciative, albeit slightly weary, smile that definitely involved those killer eyes.

What I felt like doing was giving him a lung-collapsing Cassie-type bear hug! Instead, I wrapped my arms around myself and twirled. I was even more excited now than I'd been at the very beginning of our project. James had good broad shoulders; well-developed biceps; hair that was looking fantastic, thanks to Raphael's magic with a pair of scissors; passable ears; and, now that his teeth were whitened, an excellent smile. But James had eyes that knocked a person right into the central hall. They were possibly the best eyes at Fairport! What a perfect finish to our makeover!

"The eyes have it!" I proclaimed. "James!" I turned to him quite suddenly. "I've changed my mind about your new glasses. I don't want you to wear them at all."

"But I need glasses to read."

"Okay, wear them just when you read. When you walk down the hall, keep them in your pocket. Once the girls discover your eyes, we've got the female vote at Fairport!"

This was too much for James. He plopped into a corduroy chair, sighed, and shook his head. It was no time to pout and I didn't let him get away with that. "Let's celebrate!"

I pulled James up and started dancing with him. Cassie hooked on to the back of James, and then Derrick held onto her sash and started doing a derivative of the funky chicken. Terrance latched on to Cassie and started moving his arms in a kind of hokey pokey. Garlie looked like she was planning to keep holding up the wall as she chewed the end of a pencil. I pulled her in, took away her pencil, and pushed her toward Bud. Their vast contrast in height made them quite the striking duo.

My brother pulled Sadie away from the computer. "Come on, Sadie, my Lady," he said, dipping her to the floor. Did she ever snort that time! Next Alex pulled a couple of newer committee members into the action—Lotus Leaf Malouf, and Larry Lagardi, better known as Larry the Lard. Had he been fifty or so pounds heavier, he could have been Cassie's other bookend.

Alex and I smiled at each other because Adriana was staring at all of this in amazement. "I hope you're not one of those double agents," I joked as I danced by her, "because there's some juicy action going on here that Carson and Lyla's troop would probably really relish hearing about." It was true. This was a regular geek-dork fest we were hosting.

Adriana laughed. "Yeah, I'm just wondering who's transforming who here?" It was her way of letting me know that Alex and I were beginning to act as if we fit right in with this *unusual* group of people. And maybe we did! Strangely, at that moment, it didn't matter. The following day was the election and after that things would get back to normal. Yes, it would all be over soon, but right now we were having a pretty good time.

Adriana watched us for a while, fascinated, and then apparently decided she didn't care that much either. With an "aw, what the heck" expression, she hooked on to the back of Lotus and started doing a combination hokey pokey and funky chicken.

— 👓 —

I can't remember going home that night, but we must have. I can't remember inviting the committee to meet at James's that Friday afternoon after the primary election either, but Alex and I were there along with everyone else. I told myself we were there to comfort James and that we should prepare for the worst. I told the others that too. But it was obvious by the anticipation in their eyes that, like me, they were hoping beyond hope that there really was such a thing as a miracle. And then the phone rang.

"How'd it go, Buddy? . . . What? No kidding?" Alex turned in our direction, but then jerked back to the phone. "Wait, let me make sure I heard you right. Repeat that." When Alex turned to us again, his face had lit up like a Christmas tree. He turned back to the phone one more time. "You're not pulling my chain, right?"

"Tell us!" I almost shouted as we closed in on Alex.

Alex pulled the phone from his mouth. "James made the finals!"

"Is this a joke?" I grabbed the phone from my brother. "James? James, you're really in? Oh, my stars, you're really in the finals?"

"That's what they're telling me," James said, his voice cracking a little.

"It's true!" I turned to the others, laughing, almost crying. "It's honestly true!"

"Whoopteedoopteedoo," Derrick crowed.

Terrance began pummeling a couch cushion. "Whooeeee!" He pummeled it again.

What Cassie shouted is, of course, no mystery.

Garlie and Bud started swing dancing. Sadie pushed her hair from her face, stretched out her arms and flapped them.

I didn't bother to ask James who else had made it to the finals. Lyla had run a brilliant campaign. But that James had defeated popular people like Marla Lopez, Lucas Hart, and Jacey Pruitt was beyond imagination. I grinned and clapped my hands together. It would take more than a miracle to beat Lyla, but right now that didn't matter. We'd made it to the finals! Maybe Lyla thought it was over, and maybe it was, but we were in the finals! Even if we lost in the end, we'd gotten this far and that in and of itself was miraculous and seemed to legitimize all our efforts.

I sat down on the couch and narrowed my eyes. But we weren't finished yet. Oh, no, we had much more to do. Maybe our chances were slim as far as really winning, but I'd personally see to it that

Lyla Fannen would remember this race. Oh, yes, she'd know she'd run against *us!*

"Okay!" I stood up again. "Okay, we have a lot of work to do and there's no time to waste!" I knew that the biggest vote-getter would be the finalist speech coming up the following Wednesday. Those short speeches would determine the winners and the losers. "Derrick, Sadie, I have another computer assignment for one of you. We've got to work on James's speech right now! Alex, where's Alex?" Alex was standing in the corner, punching the wall and laughing to himself. "Come here, Alex . . . Adriana, any chance you'd have time to help us brainstorm?" This needed to be a joint effort because this speech needed to be absolutely perfect: funny, clever, a real attention-grabber. "The celebrating is over," I announced. "Let's get back to work!"

Chapter Seventeen

I'd really like to keep this speech simple and straightforward," James reminded us again on Monday.

"Uh-huh." I was tired and annoyed and I just didn't want to hear it anymore. On Wednesday morning he would be standing on the auditorium stage in front of the entire student body and we weren't even close to having his presentation ready. The second he stepped up to that microphone, it would no longer be enough for James just to *look* good. He needed to *sound* good as well. This speech would need to leave no doubt whatsoever in anyone's mind that James really was Super-Jim, Fairport's next president.

"It's past time I present my ideas for the school to the students," James continued. "They need to know what I stand for."

We'd heard that before too. "Yes, of course," I said, "but like I've told you, it's also essential that this talk be clever." As a matter of fact, we were working on our fourth draft of *clever* because *clever* can be elusive. What sounded extremely clever and funny one day came across with a dull thud the next.

James was scowling again. "I want to talk about making our school a place where every student feels comfortable and welcome. A place where learning is easier because people care about each other. I have several things listed that I want to cover."

"You bet!" I said, taking his list from him and handing it to Sadie. "Sadie, why don't you type that in."

"Okay," said Sadie with a snort.

I planned to edit it out later.

"What about that costume, James?" I asked, trying to distract him. He'd emphatically turned me down twenty minutes before, but I was hoping he'd changed his mind about wearing Superman tights and a cape. Even though skits had been eliminated this year—thanks to a couple of committees who'd chosen obscene subject matter the year before—props were allowed and several of the candidates were dressing up. I turned to Alex and Adriana. "Help me talk James into this," I pleaded with them.

"We've already talked about this," said our normally easy-to-work-with candidate with great firmness in his voice. "No tights!"

"I don't think he's budging on this," said Alex. Under his breath he added, "And I don't blame you, Dude."

"Fine." I sighed. Alex was right. James had made up his mind on the costume and there really wasn't time to argue anymore. Besides, I wasn't a hundred percent sold on the idea myself. Granted, James's arms looked great now and his chest was more than adequate, but for all I knew his legs could be pogo sticks. "Okay, then let's move on."

But James was not moving on. "Sergei?" James addressed the newest committee member, a friend of Derrick's. "What are some things you're hoping will happen in our school next year?" When Sergei studied the floor with embarrassment, James lowered himself next to him and began to ask him questions. James listened to the Russian boy's ragged answers attentively until he became rather animated. "Those are good ideas," James said.

Next James turned to Lotus Leaf, then Cassie, then Garlia. He asked each committee member to express his or her feelings and thoughts. I watched, intrigued at his thoughtfulness, and found myself amused and even impressed by the fairly insightful responses. But then I shook my head like a wet dog. We had work to do!

Alex, Adriana, and I worked on James's presentation until midnight that Tuesday night. To our surprise Sadie came up with some decent input as well. She suggested we do something with the famous phrase: "Faster than a speeding bullet, more powerful than a locomotive, able to leap tall buildings in a single bound . . ."

"And then there's the part about 'fighting for truth, justice, and the American way,'" she added quietly. "We could put some of that in but change it to fit with the election and our school."

I stared at her. "That's pretty good. That's honestly not a bad idea, Sadie."

Sadie moved back a little in the computer chair and sniffed with satisfaction.

By the time we'd finally finished with the speech, committee members were strewn across James's living room. Terrance Dokey was snoring in the corner, his mouth wide open, his arms close to his sides. He jerked when I tapped him on his shoulder. Alex pulled down Bud's arm, and I nudged Cassie, who was taking up the entire corner next to the couch. Garlia had left at about nine to meet some of her scary friends at some equally scary hangout down by the lake. Derrick and Sergei and some of the newer committee members had followed Garlia out to the sidewalk to say good-bye, but thankfully returned to help us finish James's presentation.

Tomorrow's the big day, I thought, looking around. *We're almost there!*

— ❦ —

"This is a clever talk, and I appreciate all the effort, but I don't see the information here that I wanted to include," James objected very early Wednesday around six A.M. after he'd read the speech we'd finally finished putting together for him. "I'm going to need to add a few things."

I immediately panicked and opened my mouth to object, but Alex beat me to it. "Trust us on this," he said, patting James on the back. "This speech is a winner! Later you can present your ideas and say whatever you'd like, but first we need to get you in."

"That's right," I agreed, greatly relieved that my brother and I were eyeball-to-eyeball on this. "If you get up there and present some kind of completely serious presentation, you won't get in and then it won't matter what lofty goals you have for the school. It's really important that you give the speech as we've written it word for word. Alex and I will be right up front plugging for you." It was absolutely essential that James stick with the exact words we'd come up with. "Now let's practice!"

Chapter Eighteen

romptly at 10:00 on Wednesday morning, Alex and I were
sitting in the middle section of the high school auditorium
on the front row just as we'd promised James we would. I
could hear Sadie behind us, wheezing heavily. The candidates,
seated on the stage on folding chairs, fidgeted, cleared their
throats, and studied their notes, their props under, behind, or next
to their chairs.

After Max Pierce, our current president, had gotten everyone's
attention with a few corny jokes, he said, "This is the day you've
been waiting for!" Max introduced the candidates, informing us
of the order in which they would be speaking. I was gratified at the
nice reaction James received when he stood. Cassie, of course,
cheered with full lung capacity, and the others on our committee
weren't exactly keeping quiet either, but it was obvious by the
degree of volume that it wasn't just our committee members cheering for James. I elbowed Alex and lifted my eyebrows. We weren't

surprised, of course, when a few seconds later, Lyla received a much stronger response.

The finalists for historian spoke first. Yolanda Marsh, who sang her speech, was the obvious winner. Yolanda had been a runner-up in a recent local version of *American Idol* and sounded very similar to Alison Krauss. "You go, girl!" somebody shouted.

It was obvious that poor Mark Armor didn't have a chance, even though somebody—I guessed his mother—had gone to a lot of trouble to make him an impressive shield, sword, and helmet.

Ruby Backus, complete with ruby slippers, stuck with her *Wizard of Oz* theme. "We'll follow the yellow brick road to a magical year!" she proclaimed.

Caroline Yang, who was running against Ruby for treasurer, read a fake resume in which she claimed she'd been asked by Alan Greenspan to head a committee on national school finances. She listed several other great achievements and then pulled out a large bill and stated that in honor of all she'd done, the president of the United States had recently authorized the use of her picture on the new forty dollar bill. She received some applause and a decent response.

It looked as though it would be a close race as well between John Carlisle, who continued the play on his first name with his "outhouse" theme, and Salina Daniels, who got everybody clapping with her Fairport rap.

Brad Jenkins—"Be rad! Vote Brad!"—gave us the top ten reasons we should elect him vice president. "And the number one reason you should vote for me," he concluded, "is because if I win, I will shave my head, paint it blue and gold, and wear it that way my entire senior year." Most of the students stood and cheered. It appeared to me that Brad had already won and that Lola Fisher's fishing pole wouldn't be reeling her in enough votes to offset those Brad had just gained.

During all the talks I was bouncing my books on my knee and squeezing my fingernails into my French textbook. At last it was time for the presidential candidates to give their speeches. I gripped the armrest tightly, readying for the ride. "Okay, James, you can do this," I whispered. But first I narrowed my eyes at Lyla, who would be speaking first.

Lifting a milk carton and smiling her whitened smile, Lyla Fannen rose gracefully and walked to the microphone with great confidence. She had every reason to be confident. The previous week virtually hundreds of students had passed out fliers asking, "Got Lyla?" Although it was ironic in the sense that the majority of her committee members preferred Jack Daniels to milk, I begrudgingly had to admit that having the cool people of the school all sporting milk mustaches was a highly effective and clever attention-getter.

But apparently Lyla felt that James had generated a little too much attention with his makeover. Or maybe she was unhappy with the amount of applause he'd received. After she'd said a few words that corresponded with her "Got milk?" theme, Lyla suddenly turned the milk truck around, so to speak, and started after *us*.

"You've probably noticed that my opponent has made some changes over the last weeks," Lyla said. "Together we've watched James transform into . . ." she paused, "Super-Jim?"

I noted the question mark and pulled back in my seat with concern as a few audience members clapped uncertainly. Lyla adjusted the microphone. "But how much has he *really* changed?" The clapping died down as Lyla put her mouth even closer to the mike. "You can change somebody's outward appearance," she warbled sweetly, "but you can't change who he really is. Are we sure our new Super-Jim isn't just the same old . . ." Lyla's mouth pressed against the microphone as she whispered, "dork?"

Lyla pulled back in mock surprise. "What did I say? Did I really just call my opponent a dork?" She opened her eyes in fake innocence. "Well, shame on me." Lyla tapped herself charmingly on the cheek, then flashed her beautiful smile and leaned in close again. "Or is he more of a geek?" Audience members began to titter. "I guess the question is this: Do you want to vote for somebody's . . . *project* . . . or the well-established Lyla Fannen?" She held up the milk carton again.

"Get Lyla! Get Lyla!" a group near the middle of the auditorium began chanting. Five or six football players in the right section stood up, cheering. Carolee Jeffries and Isabelle Schmidt from the drill team jumped up and started line dancing. Soon it seemed as if everyone in the entire auditorium was chanting "Get Lyla!"

James squirmed in his seat on the stage and wiped his fingers across his brow. *Settle down,* I tried to telepathically e-mail him. *Don't lose your courage.* Another part of me was thinking, *Just give up now because it's over.*

When James stopped squirming, I assumed he'd gotten my first message. Then I noticed that his eyes were shut and his mouth was moving ever so slightly. He was praying! I honestly couldn't blame him. *If I believed in prayer, I'd be praying myself right now,* I remember thinking.

When James opened his eyes, it was as though a transformation had taken place. He looked down at Alex and me and smiled confidently. I raised my eyebrows at Alex with relief. James seemed to be all right and I knew why. I was certain my friend had just put his fate in his Lord's hands. For once I didn't mind. This time it was absolutely fine with me if he carried that Dumbo feather to the microphone with him. Whatever gave him the required confidence and courage was fine with me!

I placed my hands together and pressed them tightly against each other. But my knee was jerking up and down as if it were a drill now, and I was pecking into the air worse than Derrick.

Please, James, I thought, *just stick to the speech.* If James repeated the exact words we'd written for him and kept his voice low and his enunciation clear, he would at least not crash and burn before our eyes. Yes, if he stuck to the words like super glue, we would still be all right. The speech was, after all, a work of art. If James handled himself the way we'd practiced, everything might still work out for us. Even if he lost the election, he'd at least come away with some degree of respect from the students.

As our friend rose from the chair, I rose ever so slightly along with him. *Stand up straight,* I mouthed. James immediately lifted himself to his full stature. It was exactly like the scene in the old *Superman* movie. *Yes!* But he was still wearing his glasses! *Your glasses! Your glasses!* James either read my mind or my lips once again. He took off his glasses and slipped them suavely into his pocket as he moved along the row of candidates toward the micro-phone. *So far so good!* James was doing well!

How was Lyla handling this? I glanced her way and saw one of her eyebrows lift and her mouth pull down to one side. I narrowed my eyes in suspicion. Something didn't seem right. Was she up to something? My heart jumped to my throat when I saw Lyla push her Louis Vuitton bag into James's path.

With a gasp, I leaned forward, partially rising out of my seat again, but it was too late. I watched in horror as James tripped over the bag and stumbled forward. He made a valiant effort to regain his footing, but at last he just couldn't catch himself, possibly because somewhere in there, Lyla had managed to stick her foot out as well.

I could only watch helplessly as, seemingly of its own volition, James's body continued moving forward. It became obvious from the angle and the speed he was moving that gravity was going to prove the winner in this scenario. Our friend was going down. With a huge thump, James Orville Wickenbee hit the stage floor.

Noooo! I gasped, fell back in my seat, covered my eyes, grabbed my brother's arm, then uncovered my eyes. Was he okay? James lifted his chin and looked up at the stage lights above, seemingly dazed and disoriented.

The auditorium was deathly quiet. Then some smart aleck sliced into the silence by shouting, "Have a good trip?" Lyla took full advantage of the moment by lifting her hand as though to say, "See? What did I tell you? He's no Super-Jim!" But then she came up with an even better idea. Lyla stood up, placed one foot on James's waist, and raised her arms in victory.

Her action seemed to delight the students of Fairport High, who laughed and cheered like fans at a pro wrestling match. Mrs. Hamilton, the vice principal, moved quickly to the microphone. "Please, students," she pleaded as teachers and assistants motioned for everybody to settle down. "There's no humor in someone's misfortune."

President Max and Mrs. Hamilton hurried toward James to help him up. Some of the candidates rose and moved forward, but only Ruby actually reached down to aid James. With the help of Yolanda, Lyla quickly gathered up the milk carton and other items that had flown from her bag.

"What a loser!" I heard from a couple of rows behind us.

Make that plural, I thought, slumping down into my seat, my hand over my mouth. I felt as if I'd just fallen down with James. This was a nightmare! Next to me Alex was standing, trying to determine whether he should jump up on the stage to aid his friend. Had I looked down the row, I'm sure that Dokey's mouth would have been hanging open wide enough for a diesel to roll in and that Derrick would have been pecking into the air with the speed of a drill. Behind me Sadie was wheezing and snorting with such intensity that it sounded as if she was planning a liftoff. Cassie was groaning. When a friend of Garlia's—a tall, skinny guy with multi-colored hair—laughed raucously, I saw Garlia elbowing him hard in the stomach.

Just when I thought things couldn't possibly get worse, they did. In trying to aid James, Mrs. Hamilton slipped on stage, landing in a highly unflattering position across James's legs. Max did his best to assist her but was almost pulled down himself. Finally, with the additional help of Ruby and John, Mrs. Hamilton was able to flip her legs into a workable position, but not until we'd seen London and France, as they say. James was making an effort to lift himself as well.

Stay down, James! Roll over and play dead.

But James did not stay down. In spite of Max, Mrs. Hamilton, and the others, he managed to pull himself to his knees, then to his feet. Limping only slightly and stretching his arm, he moved toward the microphone, where he waited patiently for everyone to calm down. That took almost a full minute.

I stared at the stage as Max helped Mrs. Hamilton to her seat and the patrolling teachers attempted to quiet down the students. Finally James lowered his mouth to the microphone. "I tripped," he announced.

I tripped? Had he really just said, "I tripped?" I hoped beyond hope that nobody past the first row had heard him say, "I tripped."

James moved closer to the microphone, intent on making sure everyone heard what I considered a truly strange and even asinine statement. "I tripped," he repeated, louder.

I turned to Alex. "Hello! I think we all know he tripped. What's he doing?"

Without moving his eyes from the stage, my brother lifted his shoulders and shook his head slightly, his eyebrows knit together.

It had quieted down a little, but unfortunately, it appeared several students had heard James's announcement. "He says he tripped!" someone a few rows behind us shouted.

"News flash!" somebody else jeered.

I sunk down even lower in my seat, breathing heavily, almost gasping, my eyes burning. Why on earth didn't James just give his speech? *James, please. Move on and move on fast. Your speech. Read your speech! Oh, please start it now. "Truth . . . justice" . . . your speech . . . come on! Pleeeeezeeeee!*

"I know what you're thinking," James continued as though he hadn't heard the jeers. "You're thinking that a superhero wouldn't trip. You're thinking that what Lyla said must be true: You can change someone's appearance, but you can't change who he really is. You're thinking: This guy is no superhero."

"You got that right!" somebody yelled.

"Yes," James said, pointing to that somebody, a sophomore with a tuft of hair that shot straight out of the top of his head like an erupting volcano. "Yes, I did get that right, Eric."

The surprised sophomore stood for a second or two longer, looked around, then sat down. Others stopped jeering as well, and it was soon evident that most of the students were listening.

"And so did Lyla," James continued. "Lyla Fannen, my opponent in the race for president of Fairport High, got that right."

Lyla? Why mention Lyla? Why didn't he just give his speech? What was he doing? I bit my lip and clutched at Alex's arm again.

Alex apparently still didn't know where James was going with this either because he sat stone still, staring forward. Across the stage, the candidates looked confused. John Carlisle's eyes narrowed in puzzlement, his head cocked to one side; Brad and Yolanda leaned forward; Ruby and Salina lifted their eyebrows in surprise. Lyla, who had her mouth open, quickly shut it and looked around her.

"I may look completely different than I did a few short weeks ago," James continued, "but inside I'm still James Orville Wickenbee, the guy from Idaho who doesn't care all that much about his clothes or his appearance. You're right, Lyla, I'm still the geek in the glasses."

"Geeks rock!" somebody, probably a geek, shouted from the balcony. It seemed to surprise everyone and a soft wave of laughter rippled through the audience.

"Now I have to say that my friends tried. They did what's known as a makeover on me, and I appreciate their help. When I stand up straighter, I do look better. And my hair . . . you like my hair? Somebody named Raphael cut it. That is Rrrrr-aphael. You have to roll the R when you say it. But Lyla, again, you're right. This haircut, these clothes? None of this was my idea."

"My big mistake," James continued, "was taking off my glasses. If I'd been wearing them"—he turned and looked at Lyla—"I might not have tripped over your bag, Lyla. But I don't blame any-body but myself." I raised my eyebrows at Alex who raised his eye-brows back. A corner of his mouth was lifted.

"So . . ." James flipped his glasses out of his shirt pocket and put them on. "If you elect me president, I promise to wear my glasses so that I can continue to see clearly what's required to make Fairport the best school possible." A few people clapped when he slipped the glasses onto his nose. To my relief they were his new glasses.

"I have a few notes here on what I, James Orville Wickenbee, have in mind for our school. And maybe it'll help you understand exactly who I really am and what I stand for. Because even though

I don't care that much about clothes or hair, there are other things I really do care about."

Okay. I could almost breathe again. I looked around as James proceeded to outline carefully his plans for the school. He covered just about everything he'd been telling us all along that he wanted to say in his speech. The heckling stopped and students were listening. There was no way this could be working, but it was.

"I see a school where students care about each other," James finished. "I see a school where everyone without exception feels comfortable and accepted no matter what his or her race, financial state, social status, or religion. I see a school where not a single student feels like a loser whether he's from the Fairport Heights area or a trailer park behind the Wal-Mart." James took off his glasses. "As some of you know, I don't drink, but nevertheless, I lift my glasses to Fairport!" James stretched his arm upward. "Here's to every Clark Kent out there! Here's to you if *you've* ever tripped and fallen! Here's to you if you've ever felt like a loser! Here's to a better school and better feelings between us because, in reality, there's no such thing as a loser! There are no losers at Fairport High—only winners!"

I'd never seen James quite this animated. Oh, he'd come close to this level when he'd shown me his chemistry experiments, but he was outshining even his performance that day. I was mesmerized.

The same sophomore who had stood before jumped up again and lifted both arms. James pointed to him and he pointed back as others began applauding. Grinning, James pointed to Cassie and Bud and then Derrick and Dokey. I don't know if he found

Sergei or Lotus or any of the other newer members who'd helped on the committee, but I think he saw Garlia and pointed to her. Lastly, he pointed to Sadie and Alex and me.

"I'm going to be walking back to my seat," James said when everyone had quieted down. "Let's pray I don't fall on my face again. But if I do, I'll get up. And we can all do that. We can keep getting up until together we lift this school, our own Fairport High, to new heights!"

The students of Fairport High clapped and cheered loudly. They seemed to be elated that Super-Jim had gone back to being just plain old James Orville Wickenbee. Most of all, I suspected, they liked the part about there being no losers at Fairport High School.

I looked around still amazed and laughed a little. Alex was chuckling and looking around as well. Terrance Dokey looped his arms around our necks and bumped our heads together. "Wowsers!" Cassie felt the need to shout right in my ear.

"Where did he pull that from?" I asked Alex. "Did you know he had something like that in him?"

"I thought I knew James pretty well," my brother answered with a chuckle, "but I'm as surprised as you are." Alex turned and high-fived Bud and then Derrick.

"He might even have surprised himself," I said with a giggle.

"I have the strong feeling that our buddy got a little help from up there," my brother said, pointing ceiling-ward.

I didn't argue with Alex, first of all because I was far too happy and secondly because I'd just recognized the need to quickly brace myself. Cassie had hugged everybody on her row and was heading around to Alex and me. "You know, Alex, this just might be a much closer race than anybody would ever have expected," I stated as I anchored myself to the back of the seat.

"He's gonna win!" Cassie shouted as she lunged at us.

— ꝏ —

About twenty minutes later, as I headed to my locker, Dolly Devonshire, Lyla's friend and our old lunch partner, hurried up to me. Her top covered a little more skin than usual, but not a great deal more. "Oh my gosh, I think James might have a chance. He's so sweet, so different now, but still sweet. It was so cool what he said. He's right, I feel like a goofus myself sometimes."

"You *are* a goofus," I heard myself say.

She stared at me.

"I mean we're all goofuses deep down, aren't we?"

That seemed to make her feel better. "Do you need anybody else on James's committee?" Dolly asked.

I raised my eyebrows. "I thought you were on Lyla's committee."

Dolly pushed her lips forward and for the first time I saw the indication of intelligent life in those pale eyes. "I think James would make a better president," she said.

Chapter Nineteen

E verybody wants to know. Was James ever really a dork?" It was Christa Morningdove, my sophomore year debate partner, who first asked me the question. "I don't know anybody who knew him before he ran for president, but when he first ran and he wore those strange clothes and those really strange glasses . . . You and Alex put him up to that, right? Oh, and then the speech? Was it all planned that he trip and fall?"

"What do you think? Do you think it was all staged?"

"I do." She smirked and nodded. "I think you planned the whole thing." But then she paused. "Right?"

Had it been staged or hadn't it? Students all over the school were speculating. After all, how could someone who had been until oh-so recently one of Fairport's nonentities, rise up to be its most prominent student, the head of its student government, the king of the school?

Yes, in a major upset, James won the presidency of Fairport

High. Lyla Fannen? She skulked off like a peacock with broken tail feathers. Did I feel sorry for her? Not in the least. In fact, I stayed on my guard expecting her to recover extremely quickly and soon be doing her best to undermine James's efforts.

The Saturday after the election James and I played chess again just like we had every Saturday almost all year. Our weekly game was still a stabilizer in my life and seemed to help James relax as well. "You won," I said, after he'd checkmated my king. "That's twice this week."

James looked up from the board and lifted one corner of his mouth. He knew I was talking about the election and that it was my low-key way of saying congratulations. "*We* won," he said.

James really does have class—genuine, from the core, class, I remember thinking. *The kind of class you can't hide even with bad clothes and a poor haircut.* I found it highly satisfying that the students of Fairport had recognized that. It gave me a great deal of hope.

James's classiness was once again confirmed that following week—the last week before the chess tournament. Even though he had to have felt overwhelmed with all his new responsibilities as president elect, James took the time to play extra games of speed chess with me to help me review and prepare. And undoubtedly because my friend was preoccupied with these other concerns, I finally defeated him in a game.

"Good job!" James said. "Impressive!"

I respected him for not falling off his chair in amazement and I let him know that.

"No, you're really good," he said. "In fact, I wouldn't be surprised if you kick you-know-what in the tournament!"

"Kick what?" It seemed like an uncharacteristic thing for James to say and I wondered if he would complete the thought.

"You know."

"No, tell me," I insisted.

James chuckled and reddened.

I giggled a little with excitement myself because, thanks to him, I was well-prepared for the chess tournament and I'd been looking forward to what I hoped would finally be my own personal claim to glory.

And then, as though it were a dream, I was sitting at a tournament chessboard in the Cleveland State library. I moved piece after piece, from my pawns to my knights, until finally I did kick "you-know-what" at the matches that week.

I qualified for regionals, where I defeated the skilled Frieda Lamboon and then, with some marginal effort, I defeated Jed Garcia, who'd won the year before.

It wasn't until the semifinals that I lost to an irksome little freshman newcomer with droopy eyes and braces named Charles Roybal. A bit too confident by then, I grew impatient and made a truly stupid move that gave Charles's knight access to my queen and ultimately his queen to my king. The instant I'd pulled my thumb and index finger from that bishop, I knew I'd made a huge error, but there was no going back.

I did feel a little better when I found out afterwards that measly Charles Roybal had an extremely un-measly IQ and was your basic boy genius. There'd been an article about him in the

Cleveland *Sun,* according to Adriana. I felt somewhat vindicated as well when Charles ended up winning the state championship. I was also not surprised. Charles was the first opponent I'd played who I thought might actually have a chance against James.

"So are you all right?" James asked after the match.

"I'm all right," I said. "There's always next year." It was funny how amazingly all right I really felt.

I analyzed it that night and realized that it came right back to the election. Nothing—not even winning the Teen to Young Adult Ohio State Chess Championship—could top the satisfaction of having helped James win the presidency of Fairport High— nothing. I wondered if there would *ever* be anything that would top that highlight in my life. Never would I have guessed that within a few short months, I would seriously be wondering just how glad I was that I'd help catapult my friend to leadership, prestige, and popularity.

— ∞ —

All that summer James planned his presidency, or his "stewardship," as he called it. He outlined in great detail his hopes and aspirations for the school, met with other student body officers, and coordinated plans with the faculty. He was one conscientious and busy president elect! But still he scheduled time to play chess with me weekly.

"Jana," he said on a Saturday afternoon in July as he lifted one of his white knights. "I meant what I said in my campaign speech. I really want to make a difference at Fairport and I really hope to help our classmates lead better, more productive and meaningful lives. You won't be sorry you helped me become president."

"You're boring, James."

He grinned, but then his face once again turned earnest. "Do you mind if I run some things by you that I'm hoping to see happen in our school?"

"Of course not." What else could I say when James was positively trembling with excitement?

As my friend began to outline his plans for the school in greater detail than he ever had before, I wasn't surprised at how meticulously he'd thought everything through. Still, they remained extremely idealistic aims.

"I want people at Fairport High to feel real joy inside," he said after a few minutes. Had his intensity been a light bulb, it would have lit up the room. "The students in our school look for happiness in all the wrong places. They hang out and party all the time, but they always seem to be searching for something they'll never find in drugs or alcohol or immoral activities. I'm hoping I can help our classmates see that there's a big difference between temporary pleasure and real joy and convince them that you can have a great time without detouring into dangerous territories. Jana, I want this to be the best year of their lives so far."

"Well, good luck, Don Quixote," I responded, my voice coming out a bit more gently than I'd planned. The truth is I couldn't help admiring James's extremely lofty and ambitious goals and I think he knew that. I was rooting for the guy. But then a concern that I'd been harboring ever since James had been awarded the Fairport presidency resurfaced and I looked up. "You're not thinking of trying to convert everybody to your church, I hope. Please assure me you're not going to attempt to . . . *Mormonize* everyone."

"You mean am I going to proselyte? I'm not going to get up in front of the school and preach to the students if that's what you mean. But I *do* want to convert our classmates to living lives that are worthwhile and good."

I pointed at him with the rook I was holding and lifted my chin. "Just keep in mind that you're the president of Fairport, not its bishop."

Chapter Twenty

ᑐᗞ

They're sheep," I said to Alex several weeks into our senior year. "I'm telling you, the students at Fairport are all mindless sheep."

During our junior year at Fairport it had been social suicide to indicate in any way that you might have values. Now, under James's tutelage, morality seemed to be making a comeback. Yes, it was obvious things were moving in an entirely new direction at Fairport High. Even I wasn't sure how James had managed it. Almost overnight it had become acceptable to act self-disciplined, moral, and even kind. Still, as he'd promised me, James didn't preach. He was just . . . himself. In his quiet, respectful manner, he presented ideas in such a way that his words touched the hearts of the students of Fairport. Oh, he hadn't accomplished this all by himself. I think it was actually Ruby Backus who started the Respect Yourself through Abstinence campaign. A few of the jocks complained and criticized the program but other than that the program was astoundingly well-received.

Just before the homecoming dance in late September James proclaimed, "I don't think the students of Fairport High need drugs and drinking to have a good time." He challenged us to test this concept by celebrating homecoming clean and sober. Amazingly, only a few diehards slipped out of the dance to "booze it up."

When Missy Ellis, a Down's syndrome girl, was voted homecoming queen, Katrina Utley was furious. "How'd *you* like to lose to *her*?" Adriana overheard the former Lyla-nite unleash to Scott Wilkes. "It's all because of James's ridiculous kindness campaign."

Yes, that was another theme James presented. He'd suggested the first month of school be designated as "Kindness Month" and for the first time possibly in years, no undersized Fairport freshmen ended up in their lockers. Nobody glued lockers shut and I didn't see one sorry soul walking through the halls with the traditional, though unimaginative, "Kick me!" note taped to his back. None of the even worse, gross, nasty, or senseless acts we'd heard about the years before were reported either. Nobody, in essence, was shouting "Loser!" from the top of the social ladders. Kindness Month evolved into the Golden Rule, Golden School campaign. My stars, it was almost too corny to believe. But it was working. James was doing a makeover on the whole school!

Where was Lyla during all of this? Our former enemy remained curiously and suspiciously quiet. I kept expecting her to make a recovery any minute, like the monster in one of those B-grade horror movies who pops back up after you think he's finally been taken care of. I watched her carefully, staying on guard, thinking the empty-eyed, almost zombie-like way she was walking down the halls lately was all an act and that she'd strike any minute, eyes bulging. But it didn't happen. By the beginning of November the news had spread through the school like a brush-fire. Lyla was no longer a student at Fairport. Lyla wasn't even in Ohio.

"I guess she couldn't handle not being queen of the school anymore," I said to Adriana that night on the phone.

"Oh, there's way more to it than that," Adriana informed me. "I got it from a good source that Lyla's been shipped to her mother's in Florida. Then, get this, her mom immediately regis-tered Lyla into drug rehab."

Lovely Lyla, my detective friend let me know, had a not-so-lovely drug addiction. According to Adriana's source—Daffney Darnel, whose younger brother was best friends with Lyla's stepbrother—Lyla's dad had plans to run for a political office and, as Lyla's new stepmom had apparently been happy to point out, his oldest daughter was proving to be a liability. Adriana quickly dismissed a rumor that Lyla had moved because she was expect-ing triplets. "That one's bogus," she said.

"And this was the girl you wanted to hook me up with so bad?" Alex asked when I told him the news. "I think you were ready to fling me into the lake when I refused to cooperate."

"Badly," I corrected. "And who knew? You'd expect that of someone from Garlia's bunch, but not Lyla."

James's response when I told him should not have surprised me. "It's sad Lyla will miss her senior year," he said with genuine concern. "She was almost Fairport's president and now she won't even be attending here. I wish I'd had a chance to talk to her before she left."

"Remind me never to go to the zoo with you," I responded.

"Why?"

"You'd probably try to hug the boa constrictor or give the Bengal tiger a big kiss."

James remained silent, obviously still feeling sorry for someone who did not, in my estimation, deserve even a pittance of pity. The girl was a barracuda. *Let her go ahead and do drugs,* I thought after I hung up. *Let her dig a hole for herself and stay buried in it.* I realized I was whispering the thoughts aloud almost like a prayer. Good grief was *I,* in a sense, praying for someone's demise? Well, it wasn't the first time.

— ∞ —

Lyla's departure cleared the way for those who'd been intimidated by her and her friends to join with James and the other officers. Even some of the former members of Lyla's elite forces seemed to sense the direction things were heading and began flipping U-turns. In fact, so many students were playing follow the leader with James that I started becoming even more skeptical about where all this was heading.

"The golden rule is a universal principle," James reminded me when I accused him of spreading his church doctrine. "It's a moral way to live regardless of what religion you belong to."

"I still maintain the ACLU will be coming after you soon," I told him. "Let's face it, you could compile all your campaigns and mottos into just one: CTR."

James chuckled. "It does all boil down to that, doesn't it?"

I nodded slowly, but without ill will. How could anyone really complain about a school that raised ten thousand dollars for a classmate who needed a kidney transplant? I admit even I almost lost my composure when I saw Libby's mother's face when Lola Fisher, the chairman of the event, presented the check to Libby. I'd contributed a few dollars myself—the amount I'd been saving in my alabaster jar for a new windshield for Uncle Bartho's car. But who could help not getting caught up in the urgency of Libby's situation?

James and his crew became nonstop. Next our president proposed that our school become a Sub for Santa center for a battered children's home. That too hit the clear high notes in my heart.

The semester flew by as we moved from one service project to the next. "Talk to someone you haven't met yet," James suggested again over the in-school television system on the Monday morning immediately after the Christmas holidays. "Get to know someone outside your usual group of friends." I knew he was still attempting to aid the lonely students walking friendless through the high school's halls. Not that many years ago I'd been a student like that and again, I tried not to feel touched, but I couldn't help it. Of course I didn't mention this to anyone. Instead I bleated at my brother again that night.

"And our classmates will be right at James's heels for this campaign too," I said to Alex.

"Don't criticize what you haven't tried," said my brother,

running his fingers down the paragraphs of still another one of the pamphlets James had given him.

"What I haven't tried?" I reminded Alex that I'd been talking to people for months that I wouldn't have normally associated with. We still saw Cassie and Sadie and a few of the other campaign committee members monthly at the "committee home evenings" at James's. In fact, Cassie had e-mailed me just that day to let me know she'd dropped another five pounds. It'd all started when she'd complained to me about her weight.

"I don't understand it," she moaned. "I totally live the Word of Wisdom. I drink hundreds of fruit smoothies and I eat nuts and dried fruit constantly. Okay, once in a while I'll have a pastry or two but I always pick the kind with fruit filling."

I knew immediately what to suggest. "You and Bud need to switch your approaches to the Mormon health code. You go with the fresh fruits, whole grains, and structured mealtimes and have Bud eat nuts and raisins nonstop—especially the chocolate-covered kind—and drink dozens of those extra-thick drinks all day."

I assured her a smoothie once in a while was good for her as long as she didn't get carried away. "It's going to take patience," I added because I could just imagine Cassie thinking she could lose a few hundred pounds over a weekend or two and then, like James, emerge from some magical revolving door, looking "super." "This is *not* going to happen overnight. We're talking about a lifestyle change. Just don't go bulimic on me. You turn bulimic on me and I'll turn ballistic on you! And keep that body moving!" I'd offered to give her our old treadmill.

"Wowsers!" she half-shouted. "Thanks!"

"Maybe you should open your own weight-loss center," my brother said when Cassie had lost ten pounds by the following week. "Your threat and intimidation program seems to work."

"Or a makeover salon?" Ever since we'd transformed James, I'd been getting requests from people for help with their appearance. I got the distinct impression I was considered some kind of fairy godmother now, complete with a super-wand. Even Derrick Farn approached me quietly one night to ask if I could help *him* like I'd helped James. I dismissed him with, "Sorry, I'm really not into that anymore." When he turned away with disappointment, I relented and gave him a few tips. Finally I tackled the real issue. I demonstrated to him exactly how he walked around the school, pecking into the air.

"I do that?" he asked, aghast. "I look and act like a chicken?"

"I'm afraid you do." I knew I'd hurt his feelings, but he pretty much held his head still from then on. Well, at least when I was around.

Thanks to my candid and not-so-subtle remarks to Terrance as well, he began swinging his arms when he walked. At first he overdid it and looked like a windmill. Finally, he somewhat mastered the technique, but since it was obvious it would take a while to cultivate the habit, I gave him a roll of masking tape and suggested he wrap a piece of it around his wrist as a reminder. Then I said, "Maybe you should put a piece of tape across your mouth while you're at it as well."

"Why?" he asked.

"To prevent it from hanging open and inviting in bats." Yes, I was harsh as usual. But it was gratifying when I saw him walking down the hall with his mouth closed and his arms swinging almost normally. Students affectionately started calling him "Okay Dokey."

My successes gave me the courage to approach Garlia. I'm sorry to say that my unsolicited efforts to inspire her to tone down not only her look but also her act didn't go over particularly well. Garlia basically told me in so many not-so-nice words to drop dead and took off to some not-so-nice place with her not-so-nice friends. It didn't strike me as a good omen that one of them was dressed like the grim reaper.

Luckily, Sadie *did* listen when I suggested she make an appointment with an ear, nose, and throat specialist. Her doctor, apparently suspecting deeper rooted problems, suggested a therapist. Gradually, as the weeks passed, our timid friend snorted and coughed far less frequently. But her hair was still a problem.

"Open the curtains," I reminded her. "Why are you hiding?" I was genuinely concerned about this problem and even bought her some clips to hold her hair away from her face. But then the next time I spotted her, there would be those dishwater streams jetting straight down her face. Since she needed to work overtime shifts at Barnie's Bowl to pay for the psychologist, I knew she couldn't afford my hairdresser. Even I was beginning to wonder if I could afford Raphael now that he'd raised his rates. As soon as I found a less-expensive stylist who was relatively skilled, I planned to convince Sadie to come along.

So how, I wondered, could Alex say I didn't associate with those not on the old social register? Just because I didn't associate with them at school much didn't mean I didn't still deal with them. The campaign was over, and we'd had our fun. Now it was time to go our separate ways.

Chapter Twenty-One

Adriana and I had started eating lunch with some of the genuinely high-quality girls in our school who were also academically minded: Kate Burgoyne. Caroline Yang. And the beautiful and pristine Michelle Wilcox.

Michelle and I had two classes together as well and we sat next to each other in French. I felt a little guilty about the fact that I hadn't so much as nodded to Sadie, who was in our class as well. One class period while Monsieur Dubois was out of the room on another "emergency errand"—we suspected prostate problems—I noticed that Michelle was looking around with a troubled expression. "What's wrong?"

"Oh, it just bothers me that I haven't spoken to many people outside of my immediate group of friends. I was talking to James and Yolanda about it the other day and I told them that I was sure everybody in our year was just one big happy family—that we're *all* friends. James said to take a closer look and I'd probably find quite a few people who still don't feel a part of things even all these months into the year. I've started doing that and I realize that there a lot of people I don't even know."

"Uh-huh." I chewed on my bottom lip and glanced toward the back of the room where Sadie was seated with her head down, her hair covering her face as usual. "Didn't you tell me you were taking a cosmetology course?" I asked.

"I am. I'm almost finished, thank goodness. It's kept me pretty busy."

Michelle's parents were fairly well-to-do according to Adriana, but they were adamant that their children develop skills they could use to put themselves through college or fall back on in case of emergency. "Do you see the girl on the back row in the corner? In the blue sweater?"

"Sadie, right? She came with Cassie to our last stake conference." Michelle began explaining what a stake conference was until I assured her that I knew the term had nothing to do with cow meat.

"Sadie was one of the hard workers who helped James get elected last year," I informed Michelle with just a little tenderness in my voice. Sadie had been a trooper after all. "But she could use some hair help, don't you think?"

"You mean because you can't see her face?"

"Exactly. Why don't you offer her a free cut and style. I'll pay for it."

"I *do* feel bad that I didn't get a chance to talk to her when Cassie brought her to church," Michelle said, twisting around gracefully. She smiled and slipped her pencil into the pencil groove on her desk. "You know what? I think I will go talk to her!"

From my second-row vantage point, I watched Michelle glide down the middle aisle toward the back. It was a long trek because people kept stopping her, asking where she was going. Pete Greemes put his leg up as a roadblock just to be funny. I glanced nervously toward the door where Monsieur Dubois had exited, tapping my knee nervously against the desk base.

When she finally reached Sadie, Michelle extended her hand. I had to tuck in my lips when Sadie moved her hair from one eye and looked up with surprise. When Michelle returned a few minutes later, she was smiling widely.

"How did it go?" I asked eagerly.

"I couldn't see just offering her a haircut. It seemed kind of rude—like I was saying, 'You've got a hair problem'—so I just introduced myself and told her that I hoped we could get to know each other. You know, Jana, I had the strangest feeling while I was talking to Sadie. I need to tell James that he was right. I got that tingly, warm feeling inside. Thanks for suggesting I talk to her."

"No problem, sure . . ." This was getting entirely too cheery for me. "But what about her hair? Did you offer to do her hair?"

"Not yet. I invited her to come have lunch with us instead. In fact, I told her to bring along anyone she'd like. Once we're all friends we can ease into the hair issue. You don't mind if she and her friends have lunch with us, do you?"

"No, why should I mind?" I quickly faced forward. Monsieur Dubois had rushed back into the room just as quickly as he'd left and was tapping his ruler lightly on his Parisian coffee mug.

No, why should I mind if Sadie brings Cassie and who knows who else when I'm finally having nice normal lunch periods with nice normal people this year?

I pulled my vocabulary list from my folder and stared at the words. Cassie had made some progress in the weight-control department, but she still couldn't seem to grasp the importance of volume control. But then, as Warner Jenkins, at Monsieur Dubois's request, started conjugating the verb *choisir* on the blackboard, I realized that a part of me honestly didn't feel bad about what Michelle had done. A part of me was actually glad that Michelle had invited Sadie and had opened the door for Cassie and possibly other members of our old committee to join us at our lunch table. *"Mes étoiles,"* I muttered. James's programs were beginning to affect even me!

Inspired by Michelle's example, people in our French class began joining the school in making greater efforts to be inclusive. One day I heard Pete greet Alvin Aflack with a simple, "Hi, how ya doing," instead of mimicking the AFLAC Insurance commercial's duck like he usually did. I also witnessed Shereen Quinn inviting partially blind Sophie Dalebout to join her and Kylie Craig on the French geography project.

One particular morning, when everybody was mixing it up with everybody else to the point of disruption, Monsieur Dubois rose from his desk and once again tapped on his coffee cup to call us to order. But when he noticed who was visiting with whom, his normally rigid expression softened into *crème an glaise.* "I'll let you continue visiting for a few more minutes," he said in English instead of French, his voice cracking slightly. "I'm glad to see everyone getting acquainted." I had the feeling he'd never seen anything like it before.

Neither had I. In spite of my pessimistic predictions, James's programs were proving to be long-term. They hadn't disappeared or dissolved into the school furnace ducts and walls after a month or two. Instead they seemed to be taking on a life of their own.

I had to chuckle a little when Kell Black, our six-foot-seven basketball forward—who'd scored the winning basket on our first official game against the Trojans—leaned way down to the floor to pick up a pencil for self-conscious, nervous Sarah Finkler. "Thank you," she whispered in embarrassment and surprise. Then somewhere inside she found the courage to lift herself, stretch tall, and call after him, "Good game, Kell."

A few days later Dan Ravino, who generally walked around with an "I'm too cool to be bothered" look of disdain on his face, showed some genuine interest in Josh Pell's science project. "I need to get more serious about school," I heard him say. "You do any tutoring?"

I was even more dumbfounded when, completely ignoring his cousin Katrina's objections, Scott Wilkes invited Dokey and Derrick and Bud to help with the decorations for the Winter Wonderland Extravaganza. "We could use a little height," he said good-naturedly staring up at Bud, his hand over his eyebrows. "And you've definitely got that, *hombre.*"

Cassie, who tried her best to be involved in every possible school activity, was literally *thrilled* right out of her shoes when Salina Daniels invited her to head the Spring Fund-raising Committee, and I mean literally. She kicked her slip-on's up into the air shouting—not surprisingly—"WOWSERS!" One shoe did a high loop and almost landed in Jate Pingree's chili. I sighed and sank down in my chair at this display, but Salina seemed to take the reaction in stride. Michelle put her hand over her mouth to keep from laughing. Luckily when Jate saw Michelle's reaction, he chuckled himself.

When Salina asked Sadie if she'd assist Cassie with the project, Sadie mumbled an okay from beneath only slightly shorter bangs. But after the other girls had moved back to other topics, I saw her tuck her hands under her armpits and flap her arms again, a response that caused me to smile in spite of my concern that now *she* was turning into a chicken.

One afternoon four-foot-two Samantha Elbert, the smallest girl in the school, grabbed Adriana in the hall and hugged her around the middle. "I love you," she said.

"All I did was tell her I liked her fingernail polish," said Adriana, pushing back some strands of her pinkish blonde hair. "Oh, and I guess I suggested she be our head manicurist for the fashion show. I'm actually wondering if we should open the participation to plus and petite sizes so more people can be involved." Adriana and I had been working hard to collect enough clothing for the school fashion show, which was scheduled in February.

"We'd need a child size for Samantha," I said. "I doubt she'd even fit into a petite." But then I bobbled my head. It was all right with me.

— ᏏᎾ —

"So how's everything been going?" Alex asked me one night at the end of January after I'd hauled in another armload of clothing from the Encore secondhand shop. Margo Skilicorn had come up with the idea of asking stores to let us donate some of their items to the homeless after we'd used them in the fashion show. It wasn't hard to tell which they were letting us give away.

"Can you believe what's happening at our school?" my brother asked. "I'm seeing things happening that I never would have expected to see in this lifetime."

"Baaaaa," I repeated once more to Alex as I snipped off a tacky plastic rose from a not-all-that-bad jacket. "Like I said, it's unbelievable how blindly people follow their leaders." Then I shared some of the things I'd witnessed.

"It's great, isn't it?"

"It's ridiculous." I tried to sound blasé as I pulled out a skirt which I thought could possibly work for Samantha if I cut out the lowest tier or two. "There are people helping each other all over the school. I tell you it's unbelievable. It reminds me of that quote by Thoreau where he says that if a leader wears a chicken-bone necklace one day, soon everybody will be wearing chicken-bone necklaces."

Alex smiled. It's not easy to hide your true feelings from someone you once shared a *womb* with. Alex knew I was as touched and amazed by what had transpired at our school as he was. My brother and I had been reading each other's minds for just about as long as I could remember. And maybe that's why I suggested he come with me to Michelle's for a haircut. It had become pretty obvious to me that he was anxious to get to know her better.

Chapter Twenty-Two

ʚ

Dolly Devonshire, Lyla's old sidekick, was one of those who'd jumped full force onto James's "A Kinder, More Moral School" bandwagon. In fact, she'd been one of the first. Some of the jocks complained when she began coming to school in much more modest shirts, her hair smoothed down, and her makeup more subdued, but by second semester, her pants were no longer glued on and she actually had some room to walk normally. Dolly, who had worn a tight, short skirt and midriff-baring top in the fashion show the year before, chose a striking two-tone top and a mid-length, feminine skirt for ours.

The fashion show, I have to say, went superbly well. We'd gone ahead and opened up participation to girls of all sizes and I was proud of the confident, happy way they'd walked down that ramp. It's always been my contention that any height is fine as long as you stand up straight, and that's what I assured them.

"Walk tall and you'll feel tall no matter what height you are." I told them. I also helped all the participants with their posture just as I had with James. I let them know that an extra side benefit to standing straight is that you also look seven to ten pounds slimmer as well. "There are many different body types," I reassured them, "and they're all okay as long as you stay fit and healthy."

"Right, uh-huh," said Carla Panduski, who had a few pounds to lose, "but why can't I be fit and healthy and have *your* body type instead of mine?"

I smiled patiently. I'd put in a lot of time and effort into looking the way I did and I opened my mouth to preach a little about nutrition and exercise when I realized she'd turned to look in Dolly's direction. "Or better yet, Dolly," she said. "Why can't I look like Dolly?"

"Or Shereen," said someone else.

"Let's not start this," I said. "We're all better off as ourselves."

I could tell Adriana was a little put out she hadn't been mentioned and she frowned as she stared at Dolly.

Yes, Dolly had always looked as though she were bursting with good health, as they say. In fact, in the past that saying had been pretty literal as she'd looked fit to burst out of her clothing. Now that she was dressing more suitably, it was still obvious she was in good health, but she looked oh-so much more approachable and appealing. People looked at her *face* now and were actually beginning to listen to what she had to say.

"You looked beautiful in the fashion show," Michelle said to her when she stopped by our table the day after our event. "I've noticed you've been looking really nice in general now as well. I love your new look."

The others, even Sadie, agreed. In fact, Cassie agreed with so much energy that Dolly had to back up a step. "Lady, you've been looking amazing these days!" she boomed out for the entire cafeteria to hear. "Doesn't she look amazing, Jana!?"

I politely agreed. "Dolly did a good job for us last night."

"And you and Adriana did *such* a good job putting that show together, Jana!" Michelle added, repeating what she'd started to tell me when she first got to the table. "It was unbelievably well done."

"Amazing!" boomed Cassie again.

"You really did do an amazing job, Jana and Adriana," Dolly bubbled enthusiastically. "Thanks, you guys! It was really well organized and really, really fun!"

"Things ended up working out," I said. "With a show like that, you're never sure it'll all come together smoothly but luckily we had some good help. I give a lot of credit to Adriana, who actually got Talbot's to work with us."

"Wow, good job, Adriana," several people said.

My friend lifted her hand in objection. "Oh, stop with the compliments! No more!" At the same time she was doing the "tell-me-more" sign with her other hand.

I chuckled and nodded. "We'd better not tell her how great she is about five more times," I said.

The girls chuckled, but then as Dolly turned to leave, I narrowed my eyes at her with suspicion. Only an hour or so before lunch, I'd seen her at James's locker for the second time that day. Oh, she'd come to James's locker before to talk about various projects and activities—but never several times in one day.

"What's going on with Dolly Devonshire?" I asked Alex that night.

"Quite an improvement, huh?" Alex said without looking up from the calculus homework which he had once again put off until the last possible minute.

"Well, yes, but I'm wondering why she's made these major style changes."

"Probably the same reason as everyone else. She's taking the 'A Better Fairport Begins with a Better You' theme to heart," said Alex.

"I'm not buying it," I told him. It had taken me pretty much all evening to catch up on my homework myself. I hate being behind. Now I tapped my pencil. Ninety-eight percent of the female population of Fairport had been looking at James with new eyes now that he'd proven himself to be an amazingly successful and inspirational school president. The year before, yes, I'd wanted every girl in the school to take notice of James so that they'd vote for him. But that was a long time ago. The votes had been tallied and the election was long over. "You know what I think? I think Dolly's been doing this just to impress our superhero."

"Hey, people change. Accept it," said my brother.

"Not that fast, they don't."

"James did." It was getting late and, holding the pencil between his teeth, Alex reached down and untied his shoes. He sat back up, took the pencil back out, and said, "James made a switch in about thirty seconds flat."

"Well, not quite that fast." At least at the time it hadn't seemed that fast. It was true that, in retrospect, James's transformation did seem like a twirl through a revolving door, but there was a significant difference. *His* had only been a surface transformation. There'd been no changes required in regard to his inner strength and quality. In fact, I hoped beyond hope that who he was inside would *never* change.

Yet, I also recognized how challenging it had to be to continue staying humble with all the attention he'd been getting that year. It was one thing to win an election, but then to actually follow up by becoming a successful and influential leader of a huge and prestigious high school like Fairport was pretty heady stuff. How could it *not* affect a person's ego when popular, good-looking people, some of whom had once even ridiculed you, were now tuned in to your every blink.

It bothered me immensely that so many others had discovered what Alex and I had known for much longer—that there was something far beyond appearance that was exciting about James, that there was something about James that made you feel better about life and yourself. I should have known that once he became president of the school, other people would see it.

As a twin, sharing had never been a big issue for me and I knew it shouldn't become one. James wasn't *mine*. We were just good friends who had been through some interesting times together and who played chess on Saturday afternoons and okay, had some fascinating discussions about just about everything, but that was all it amounted to and everybody knew that that was all it amounted to. We'd both made it clear all along that nothing else was on the agenda and that we certainly were not an *item*. But the huge amount of fanfare and attention James continuously received was beginning to wear on me nevertheless.

I especially didn't like Dolly and her cheerleader friends pouncing on him all the time and taking up every extra minute he had. In fact, even Adriana and her friend from the dance company, Darcy Glick, were hanging around James all of a sudden. Other cute girls also turned and smiled and said "Hi" with that puppy dog look whenever he walked by. My stars! Girls were following James around the halls even more than they followed my brother! It was as though James was playing some kind of magical flute.

I felt like saying to them, "Hey, Ladies, if it weren't for me, you wouldn't even have noticed James. Do you really think you would be drooling at him with those droopy eyelids if he still looked like he did before I helped him last year?" I'd even seen Katrina Utley, of all people, nod and smile ever so slightly as she passed James in the hall a few days before. Even she seemed to be coming around! It bothered me so much that for a couple of nights I went against everything I preached and ate about three pounds of pistachio nuts and downed them with four Dr. Peppers.

— ∞∂ —

Just after the Heart to Heart Dance—where James, as usual had been the center of attention—I once again ranted to my brother about all the people who'd made turnabouts. Alex said, "Change can be good. Mom's made changes; I've made changes too."

"That's right," I snorted. "Mom's into genealogy now and has been having us haul those huge bags of grain downstairs. I tell you she's becoming positively Mormonized."

"She's not the only one," Alex said quietly. "In fact . . ." He leaned through the kitchen door and called toward the study. "Mom, come in here a minute!"

I stopped opening the package of Wheat Thins that I'd just pulled out of the pantry and tilted my head at my brother and then at our mother as she came into the room with her cup of whatever tasteless drink she'd concocted this time.

"We have something to tell you, Jana," Alex said solemnly. "I'm sure you can guess."

"What do we have to tell her?" Mom was as confused as I was but then seemed to grasp what Alex was referring to. "Oh, you mean . . ." She lifted her chin in sudden understanding. "Oh . . . yes . . . yes." She set her cup down on the counter very carefully. "Yes, we do have something to tell you, Jana."

Even now I'm not sure why I didn't immediately grasp where Alex was heading when I knew my brother as well as I did and when he and Mom had been attending all kinds of Mormon meetings and activities. They had been spreading out clues like jam on white bread. So why didn't I know what they were about to say when it was the very thing I'd been so fearful and concerned about the year before?

Granted, I'd been swamped with not only my chess studies, but the fashion show and the Future Businesswomen of America's luncheon, and the National Honor Society elections were coming up. Nevertheless I still felt I should have known.

I've recognized since that part of the reason I didn't see it coming was more than likely due to the fact that Alex and Mom had been taking lessons and having study sessions for so long that I was probably lulled into believing they would just continue on this course forever and nothing would ever come of it—that things would always remain status quo. But mostly, I suspect, I didn't see it coming because I didn't *want* to believe it was coming.

"Noooo!" I responded after Alex said the words: "We're going to be baptized into The Church of Jesus Christ of Latter-day Saints."

"Oh, honey, come here." Mom tried to hug me and Alex tried to take my arm. I took several steps back from both of them.

"She'll be okay," my brother said. "She had to know it was coming. You'll be okay," he said to me.

"Noooo," I repeated when he added that because the next few months were jam-packed with activities, they wanted to be baptized right away. The baptism was scheduled for that Thursday.

For the next few days I did all I could to talk my mother and brother out of making what I considered a huge mistake. I felt now that ignoring the situation had been my mistake and that I should have gone with my brother to these meetings to offer rebuttal. With hard-to-resist Michelle on one side and a stellar friend like James on the other, what chance had Alex had? I told him as much.

"You've got it all wrong," Alex let me know. "I'm not doing it for Michelle or James. I'm doing this because God has let me know it's true. There's no doubt in my mind. The only reason we've waited as long as we have is because we kept hoping that you'd—"

I shook my head with rapid little jerks. "Never!"

"Yes, that's what we finally realized—that there was no use waiting. And that's why we're going to go ahead and do this. And you know what I'd really appreciate? I'd appreciate your support in this decision. I'm asking you to come to the baptism because Mom would be devastated if you didn't. It wouldn't make me feel too good either."

"I hope James is happy," I said Wednesday evening to my invisible friend Uncle Bartho. "He has an entire school eating out of his CTR lunchbox. He has cheerleaders and dancers literally flipping around their lives for him. Couldn't he have left my family alone?"

Chapter Twenty-Three

I don't remember a great deal about the baptism. I remember that there were quite a few people there I didn't know and I remember that Aunt Nadine had had to carry Reggie out as he shouted, "I want to be bath-tized too!" (His affinity for water had apparently remained intact since Ruthie's wedding.) I remember that both Dolly, looking elegant in a dark navy top and matching skirt, and Shereen, looking equally beautiful in a dress that complimented her golden-brown skin, were right there in the center of the action. I remember that quite a few other people from school came and that everyone seemed genuinely happy for my mother and brother.

Several groups of people invited me to sit with them, including an attractive woman who said she was the leader of the young women in the ward, but I remained alone in the back where I could feel properly miserable. Only when I saw Mom's jubilant face when Uncle Phil lifted her from the water did my lips twist into a partial smile.

Several people chuckled when James had to lower Alex under the water a second time and this time make sure his foot got immersed along with the rest of him. That gave me an excuse to shake my head. *Trust the Mormons to be such sticklers,* I thought. *So what if his foot didn't get immersed? Would he limp around spiritually for the rest of his life?* Still, when my brother emerged the second time, I found the corners of my mouth lifting again in response to *his* jubilant face. It wasn't easy to remain upset when he and Mom seemed so happy. Nevertheless I felt an obligation to go home early in protest and deny myself cookies and red punch. And that Saturday I felt obligated to say something to James.

— ᴏᴆ —

"I thought you said you weren't going to proselyte," I snapped at James at our chess match that Saturday.

"I said I wouldn't get up in front of our school and preach church doctrine, but I never said I wouldn't share what makes me happy with my friends, especially when they ask," James replied calmly. "How can I not let close friends know what I believe and who I am?" My friend paused. "And Alex wanted to know, Jana."

You'd think with my debate training I would have been able to think of a good comeback, but what could I say when James was just telling the truth? My brother *had* wanted to know. Alex had made that clear from the first. Nobody had twisted his arm. Had James not shared the information with him, Alex would have found someone who would: Michelle, Phil and Ruthie, maybe even Cassie.

"I still wish you'd let me tell *you* more about what we believe," James added then, very quietly.

I had an odd feeling then—one of those emotional spasms you get sometimes. But who could help feeling funny inside when those clear blue eyes looked at you so sincerely and with such intensity?

"Thank you, but no!" I lifted my hand as I had several times in the past. "Please!"

Generally the only tension I felt in James's comfortable living room was when my queen or king was in jeopardy and James was once again about to defeat me, but now the tension was thick. I really wanted to be angry at James and it was irritating that I had no good reason to take it out on him.

On the way home, however, I had no choice but to quietly acknowledge again what I'd learned last year—that Alex and I were not and never had been conjoined at the brain and heart. Maybe I didn't like it, but my brother had the perfect right to his own opinions and the right to follow up on them and make his own decisions. So did Mom. *Well, so do I!* I thought as I pulled into our driveway and turned off the engine.

I had the opportunity to exercise my rights the very next day when my mother brought up the subject of the Mormon Church once again and asked—actually pleaded—with me to go to church with her and Alex. "Oh, Jana, you don't know how sad it makes me that you're not feeling this intense joy that Alex and I are feeling."

"Mom!" I said, my eyes bulging. "I'm happy you're happy, I honestly am, but how many times do I need to tell you *I'm* not interested?"

And I wasn't nearly as polite with Alex when he invited me once again to learn more. "Look, I'll say this just one more time," I told him. "I *do not* want to hear any more about it. I've told you *and* James *and* Mom before: I'm just not religious. I'm not one of those people who keeps running from idea to idea. I'm me. I'm not like Dolly Devonshire or her friends. I'm not about to investigate this or take those lessons or whatever they're called because of you or James or anyone else. I can't be one of those people who says, 'Let's see, this person impressed me, so I'll be a Buddhist! Now I like *this* person so I'll be an evangelist. Oh, he's a Jew? That sounds good, I'll become a Jew!' Remember Ida?" I asked, referring to one of Aunt Ruthie's closest friends. "Ida got baptized so much that she didn't even need to shower. I like to think I have a little more depth than Ida or Dolly."

"We're not talking about Ida or Dolly," Alex said. "We're talking about you."

"Exactly. And I'm asking you once and for all to leave *me* alone."

"Well, fine!" said Alex.

"Fine!"

"Fine!"

"FINE!" We were at it again, but this time the tables were turned.

Alex sighed and shook his head and headed for the sink, where he squirted soap onto his hands to wash off the six-layer dip that our latest kitchen helper seemed to really enjoy making. Unfortunately it was the only thing she seemed to enjoy making.

As he dried his hands on the kitchen towel, however, he asked, "Since when is Dolly taking the lessons? I'd heard Emily Fitzmeier and Lola Fisher, and even Courtney Martindale were taking them, and I know Kell and a couple of guys on the basketball team were thinking about taking them after the season's over. And oh, yeah, Sophie Dalebout's reading the Book of Mormon in Braille, I heard, but I hadn't heard that Dolly was taking the lessons."

"Maybe not right now, but wait and watch. I guarantee she will."

Sure enough, Dolly was soon taking lessons. Then, not long after she started studying with the missionaries—and this shows how much our school had changed in just a matter of a year—Dolly was elected Top Senior Girl.

"Well, turning 'religious' is getting some people places," I said to Alex the night after we heard the announcement.

"What do you mean?"

"Sticking with James's Let's Be Good, Moral, and Kind Bandwagon has done Dolly Devonshire some definite good!"

"You've got to respect her," Alex said, squeezing my expensive whitening toothpaste from the middle of the tube. "*I* do." He started brushing his teeth, but then he pulled his toothbrush from his mouth. "Maybe you're a little jealous."

"Why would you say something like that?" I asked, pulling my washcloth away from my face.

"Just a guess." Apparently Alex had also been noticing that Dolly seemed to be popping up wherever James happened to be.

"Do you think she'll come to our birthday party?" I asked, placing the cloth back on my cheek. Alex and I would be turning eighteen the following Saturday and had let it be known that everyone was invited to come help us celebrate. Dolly's attendance had been something I'd been concerned about.

"She's welcome, sure, but I doubt she'll be back from the national cheer competition. In fact Butch probably won't be at our party either."

"That's right," I said, tap dancing inside. I'd totally forgotten about the competition.

— ᗝᕽ —

That Saturday I took great care to get ready for the chess game with James. I told myself it was because I wouldn't have much time afterward before the party started. I took extra time with my hair and carefully applied my blush and mascara. I pulled out several outfits, but finally decided on my blue shirt with the blue- and purple-checked collar and my new Levis. Needless to say, I wasn't angry with James any longer.

I'd recognized almost immediately that there was nothing to be upset about. Though maybe they'd changed inside, Alex and Mom hadn't changed in ways that affected me, and my fears had never materialized. Mom was her same busy but supportive self and Alex, though definitely more focused, remained, for the most part, good old Alex. If anything, he treated me even better than he had before. And since he wasn't going into politics, I guessed there wasn't really a problem with his belonging to the LDS faith.

Neither one had nagged me about it since that first Sunday after the baptism.

And as far as James and I were concerned—we were even better friends than before.

Almost right from the moment I arrived at the Wickenbees', James and I fell into an interesting conversation discussing surnames and how they originated.

"You know, I'd better start paying attention because you're fairly decent at this game, James," I joked good-naturedly as he removed still another one of my players from the little chess stage. "Have I told you that?" James was one of the few people I could joke with about losing—*my* losing.

"Then you must be pretty good yourself because you've defeated me a few times," he said, trying to sweep his wins under the rug and act as if his genius was nothing of consequence.

I smiled and shook my head because James was being classy again. "Only because you weren't paying enough attention. The first time was just after you'd been elected; you were overwhelmed. Then I had to distract you by asking about your chemistry experiments or your plans for the school, so I actually psyched you out on two of those wins. But that's it—three times."

"But you've come close to winning about a dozen more times. And hey, if you want me to lose on purpose today as a birthday gift I can do that. I'll let you have a few of my pieces to celebrate. Do you want them gift wrapped?" He grinned, knowing how I'd react to such a statement.

I decided to throw him off stride. "No, not gift wrapped, but maybe you could put on a good enough act that I'd have no idea you were letting me win."

He lifted his chin and lowered it, knowing full well I was kidding.

"Oh, never mind, go ahead and gift wrap them," I joked.

"Okay." He lifted the bishop and wrapped him in one of the colorful napkins Mom had given Mary Jane as a gift.

"Stop it," I laughed happily. "Stop it. I'll tell you what. I'll just have a few more of these." I happily reached into the bowl of pistachios Mary Jane had been kind enough to fill for us. Cassie and I had the same weakness when it came to pistachios.

As I watched James unwrap the bishop and set him back down on the board I saw that I did actually have a chance to capture that piece. I narrowed my eyes to let James know that I knew that he was up to his old tricks by trying to help me see my next move.

"You really are trying to help me win," I said. "You know I don't like that."

He grinned and then I grinned, and I think we were both relieved things were completely okay between us again. I reached for another handful of pistachios, feeling safe and happy in the Wickenbees' living room.

Mary Jane was cutting up vegetables and tending a couple of grandchildren in the kitchen. She'd been screening James's calls as well and it made me feel important that James cut off his calls until after our chess games on Saturday evenings.

Rudolf had just come home, had taken off his shoes and every once in a while walked through the room in his mismatched socks. "Hi," I said each time.

He'd grin and raise his hand. "Hi."

I could tell he was trying to solve some physics problem.

"What are you two giggling about?" Alex asked when he dropped in after working for Phil. He and James took turns helping our uncle, who was venturing forth in his own business—something combining computers and science that they'd explained to me but that I wasn't sure I understood.

Alex didn't wait for an answer, but immediately called Michelle. Within minutes she showed up with Ruby, Salina, and Cassie, who'd brought a tray of pineapple hors d'oeuvres with little umbrellas she'd been trying to perfect for the spring luau fundraiser.

"Happy birthday!" she shouted.

Ruby explained that Sadie had had to work at Barney's, but Cassie must have called Bud and Derrick because soon they were there. Sonja Paulos dropped by with Emily Fitzmeier to ask James's opinion on their flyers for the upcoming election and we invited them to stay. Wherever Sonja went, John Carlisle appeared, and soon he and his friends were there as well. Alex suggested we transfer the party to our house, but Mary Jane insisted we stay and offered to make homemade pizzas. While I helped her cut green peppers, a few other guests came over, including Uncle Phil and Aunt Ruthie; they brought balloons and foot-high replicas of a chess queen and king.

"No," Alex said. "This should rightfully belong to James. He's the real chess king. I've just been observing lately."

"Oh, no, Alex, you're king today," James said. "It's your

birthday." He turned to me. "And you're definitely the queen," he said, a smile in those killer blue eyes.

And you're the emperor of good manners and kindness, I thought. It was ironic that the house I'd been embarrassed to be seen going into last year was now *the* place my brother and I preferred to be for our eighteenth birthday party. In fact, soon Melinda Challister from the newspaper staff was taking pictures of all of us and we posed happily. Sonja had her picture taken with Cassie, Garlia, who had come for a few minutes, and Ruby. Sergei, who'd slipped in unnoticed, was pulled into the picture by all four girls.

We called Mom to bring the cake and suggested she leave a note for those who might come looking for us at our house. When she showed up at the party, she had brought several more people who had stopped by our house: Kate and Caroline and Adriana and Samantha Elbert. Paul, Terrance, Robbie, and Celia Pinnock pulled up in Robbie's truck not five minutes later. Lynette even came even though Butch wasn't there. Yolanda sang for us while Cassie taught Paul to hula.

When we ran out of pizzas James and I worked our way to the kitchen to help Mom and Mary Jane cut more veggies. We talked and laughed, ribbing each other and sharing private jokes that nobody there would have understood except maybe Alex. Rudolf kept walking through the family room looking for things in his mismatched socks, trailing his pajama-clad grandchildren behind him, and visiting happily with everyone. When we came back out of the kitchen we saw that Cassie was teaching the hula to everyone.

It turned out to be not only a fantastic day, but the best birthday party ever.

Beat that, Dolly, I thought as I drove home that night, giddy and happy. I was sure James had had more fun that evening than he'd ever had in his life. I certainly had.

— ᑅᖯ —

But the following Monday at his locker, James looked like he was having a really good time with Dolly. She was undoubtedly telling him all about the cheer competition and why they'd only come in third instead of first. Dolly was at James's locker the following day as well and every day of that first week in March. I knew it shouldn't bother me to see her talking to James. So why did it?

On Friday I saw Dolly with James again, this time in the front hall talking with Ruby's sister, Topaz, who had applied to run for president of the school in hopes of taking over as James's successor the following year. Everyone speculated that with her "more of the same" platform, Topaz would be a shoo-in even without the ruby slippers that had aided her sister the year before. While there would never be another president like James, I had to admit Fairport High could do a lot worse than Topaz Backus. Right then, however, I wasn't exactly pleased about the fact that not only was Topaz bright and witty, but she had a smile almost as wide as Dolly's.

"Are we still on for chess tomorrow?" I called to James as I headed for the front doors.

"I'm planning on it!" James lifted his hand at me then returned his attention to the beautiful blondes.

"Don't forget we're meeting at my house this time instead of yours."

"Sounds good." He grinned and then *pointed*—pointed at me in exactly the way I'd taught him to point.

"We've never missed a chess appointment yet," I said quietly to myself as I walked away wondering why I couldn't shake the unsettled feeling in my heart.

Chapter Twenty-Four

S aturday started off wonderfully. The mail came about eleven and I immediately spotted the envelope I'd been waiting weeks for. I ripped it open, read the first few words, then charged into the house to tell Mom and Alex. I'd been accepted to Harvard!

"Wahoo! No kidding?" My brother jumped from his chair by the computer, bent his knees and flipped out his palms, which I slapped happily. "Good job!" He was genuinely and thoroughly excited.

Me? Oh, I was so excited I had to hold my hand across my chest and lower myself to the arm of the leather chair to catch my breath. I'd dreamed of being accepted to Harvard maybe even longer than I'd dreamed of taking the top prize in the state chess tournament.

Mom, of course, was beyond thrilled and began to do one of those Spanish flamenco dances. "I can't wait to tell the girls at the charity league and my *sisters* about this!" she said after her third olé. "Oh, my goodness! Come here, my beautiful, intelligent daughter!" She pulled me off the chair to hug me soundly. "My daughter—at Harvard!"

As I listened to Mom and Alex, I wondered how I could ever have believed that they wouldn't always be there for me and that joining the Mormon Church would change that. Nevertheless, I hurried to the phone to call James. He knew how much I'd wanted to get into Harvard and would be just as excited as Mom and Alex. But I'd only pressed half the digits in his number when I stopped, smiled, and hung up. No, I needed to see his face! He was coming over for chess in just a few hours and I could tell him in person then. Wow, would those baby blues light up!

I called Aunt Ruthie instead and then Adriana, but I made her promise not to spread the word for a little while. I figured she'd last an hour or two at least and by then I would have had a chance to tell James. Alex, I knew, would want to be the one to tell Michelle. I thought about calling Caroline or Kate, but found myself dialing Cassie instead. There are times when you really don't mind hearing huge outbursts of enthusiasm.

"You can tell Sadie, but that's all," I said. In her quiet way, Sadie would be just as thrilled for me as Cassie was. I realized I was being a bit narcissistic, but it felt rather good.

It was early afternoon by the time I clicked off the phone. I had just enough time to spread some leftover avocado on some toast for lunch. Then I carefully and thoroughly helped Mom clean the kitchen. My room was still in good shape, but I ran a dust cloth over my chest of drawers and vanity once more and then jumped into the shower. At 2:55 I made some lemonade, adding extra ice cubes and sugar. I even slipped some Mrs. Flannagan's Apple Turnovers into the microwave because I was certain James would want to celebrate with me. Then I smiled up at the clock. He'd be over any minute!

Two hours later the lemonade was warm; the apple turnovers were cold; and I was still waiting for James.

"James isn't coming?" my mother asked as she wiped off the counter where she'd been cutting broccoli.

"I *thought* he was."

"That seems odd. He's always so dependable."

"And punctual," I added.

"Do you think he thought you were meeting at his house like you usually do?"

"His mother was having some church people over for a meeting of the board or something, and we agreed it would be better to play here."

"Did you call and check?"

I had. Three times. "I just got the answering machine," I said.

Alex, who had gone out to run a few errands, came in the back door and stomped his feet on the mat. "Man, it's a mess out there!" As he leaned over to pull off his muddy shoes, water poured from his cap.

I stared past him through the doorway at the cloudburst. When had it started raining?

"James didn't show, huh?" my brother asked as though it were the most ordinary thing in the world.

"No."

"He hasn't called?"

"No!" I snapped.

"Sor-ry," said Alex, pulling the door shut. "We're a bit testy today, aren't we?" As Alex wrung out his jacket in the sink, I felt his eyes still on me. "You probably wanted to share your good news about Harvard with old Super-Jim. Well, I wouldn't worry about it. He's probably just run into a holdup. I'm sure he'll come."

I was glad Alex was so convinced James was still coming because *I* wasn't. I suspected my brother was right about the holdup, though I was afraid I knew *who* the holdup might be. Alex started to say something else, but Mom announced that dinner was ready. "Let's go ahead and sit down now," she said.

In the years since her recovery, Mom pushed hard for some family unifying practices—one of them being that all of us eat dinner around the table as often as possible. Now she pulled a casserole big enough to serve the Roman army out of the oven and placed it proudly before us. I think she was disappointed I didn't act more impressed.

"Grace . . ." she said, lowering herself across from us. Alex and I quickly shut our eyes as Mom turned to grab a towel to protect the table. "*Grace* helped me get this ready yesterday because she's out looking for a place to live," she continued. "I decided to add a few vegetables. You know, I think Grace is going to work out very well."

Alex and I opened our eyes as soon as we realized Mom wasn't referring to saying grace but to our newest helper, the third in the last month. Mom laughed a little when she caught on, "Oh, *grace!*

Yes, let's say grace." But then she opened her eyes again. "I wonder if they call it 'grace' in the LDS faith?"

I really didn't care. This time I did not close my eyes as Mom, in a quiet and reverent tone, asked for a blessing not only on the food, but also on all those who did not have food at that moment, mentioning in particular the people in Kenya. During the entire prayer, I leaned my chin on the heel of my hand, looking out the window at the downpour. Following the "amen" I lifted my fork and began to eat listlessly. Alex, on the other hand, downed his food with the usual gusto.

"This isn't bad, Mom," he said reaching for a second portion. "It's not bad at all."

"The broccoli is a little crunchy," Mom complained as she neatly tapped her napkin against her lips. "I should have pre-cooked it for a few minutes."

"Hey, it's better this way," said my brother. "I don't like mushy broccoli." Then he spotted my cold apple turnovers. "Are those for dessert?" No, in most ways Alex hadn't changed all that much since his baptism. Becoming a full-fledged member of the Mormon faith certainly hadn't affected his appetite.

"Sure, why not?" I said with not so much as a parsley sprig of energy in my voice. "I thought maybe we'd have a little celebration when James came over, but since it doesn't look like James will be coming over, let's go ahead and celebrate now." Considering my tone, I might as well have been suggesting we all go poke shish kebab sticks into our eyeballs.

Alex hesitated. "You sure?"

"I'm sure," I said again, without even a flicker of inflection. "You bet, go ahead."

Apparently deciding it was in his best interest to take my words at face value and not try to read between the lines, my brother placed the plate of turnovers in the microwave and pushed the timer.

I separated some of the broccoli from the rest of the chicken casserole on my plate, pushed it to the side, pushed it back, then separated several fat chunks of chicken and pushed them around as well. Where was James?

"So you didn't see James at all today?" I asked Alex as Mom left to get a new roll of aluminum foil from our new storage room downstairs.

"No . . . no, uh-uh." Alex pulled out a carton of Rocky Road ice cream from the freezer and plopped a huge scoop over his turnover. Out of compassion, he added ice cream to a second turnover and pushed the plate in my direction. "Here you go. Have at it."

"Thanks, but I'm not that hungry." I pushed the plate back toward him, reached down to the bottom cupboard to get out a Tupperware container, and with my knife and a serving spoon, carefully scraped my dinner into it.

"You hardly ate anything, Jana." Mom's voice vibrated disappointment as she returned to the kitchen, unrolling a good yard of aluminum foil for the leftovers.

"I'll eat it later."

"James still hasn't come, I guess," she said, pressing the foil around the casserole.

"No. He *hasn't.*" I stretched my eyes at the Tupperware. Wasn't that *obvious?*

"Hey, wait a minute," Alex tapped his fork into the air. "You know what? I just remembered something."

I did what he'd requested. In fact, I waited for what seemed like far longer than a minute as Alex took another large bite of his Rocky Road-smothered turnover.

He pointed the fork in my direction once again and swallowed. "I *did* talk to James this morning. I talked to him on my cell." Alex swiped underneath his mouth with his napkin. "When I was over at the gym, I called him to see if he wanted to come shoot a few hoops, but he said something about going somewhere with Dolly and her friends. There was a lot of static on the line and I couldn't really hear him that well." Alex shared this information with me as though it were nothing—as though it were the most ordinary thing in the world for James to be going somewhere with Dolly and her friends on the day that he and I always, always, *always* played chess.

"What time was that?" My fears had just been confirmed and without looking at Alex, I placed a couple of glasses into the top section of the dishwasher. There was only one coffee mug there now—mine.

"It was probably about nine-thirty or ten when I talked to him. I'm not sure what time he was meeting the women." Alex had slowed down a little at the end of the sentence, looking at me slanted as he took another bite, possibly recognizing that this bit of information wasn't one I'd been hoping to hear.

I could tell he was trying to come up with something to say

that would make me feel better when somebody honked for him. Somebody was always honking for Alex.

Alex pushed the ice cream back in the freezer and hurriedly finished the last bite of turnover. My brother wiped his mouth again and ran the napkin over his teeth. It was a good thing sweets weren't on the LDS Church's forbidden foods items list, I decided.

"I'll be back in about twenty," said Alex. "I'm running with Smith and Torkinson over to the mall." He paused and looked at me. "Wanna come?"

"No, thanks."

Mom was in a hurry as well to get ready for another charity function. She too invited me to spend the evening at what she said would be a "nice affair." Again, I declined. "I'll stay home and do the dishes. Adriana wants me to come over and has some people from Westchester High coming to her house, but I'm not sure if I'll go. I really don't feel like going anywhere." I was sounding like some kind of a martyr and it wasn't Alex and Mom's fault James hadn't come, so I twisted my mouth into what I hoped resembled a smile. "I'll be fine," I said. "I'm just not in that great of a mood right now, that's all. I'll get over it."

"Would you like me to stay home with you?" Mom asked with concern, her compassion bubbling over again. "I can stay home for a change. It's not essential that I go to this function."

"No-oooo," I said with inflection on the second set of *ooo's*, "I'd just as soon you went." I didn't need a baby-sitter, thank you. "No, please go ahead."

"Are you sure?"

"Yes."

Mom hesitated, then slipped on her tan shoes, grabbed her tote, a box with flowers, a couple of books, more napkins, her tan handbag with the black trim, and with one last look of concern in my direction, finally hurried out the front door.

After I'd finished placing all the dishes in the dishwasher and had pushed the normal wash cycle button, I began cleaning the counters. They were still looking pretty good from the cleaning I'd given them earlier that day, but I couldn't think of what else to do. At first I dragged the dishrag gently across the bar, but then I began pushing it harder. I slapped the cloth in the water and swung it across the counter, smacking it against the sleek granite. I was not gentle either as I cleaned off the stove. "Dolly Devonshire," I muttered through clenched teeth.

— ∞ —

"James still not here?" Alex asked when he came back about forty-five minutes later.

"He isn't," I answered. "He's apparently busy with his *other* friends."

"Hey, I'll play chess with you. Michelle had to work tonight and doesn't get off for a couple of hours and Torkinson and Smith ran to some floral place down by Wal-Mart to get some flowers for Lynette's birthday. It's obvious Butch has a thing for her, but I wasn't in the mood to keep looking at cards. Butch had already hauled us around the entire mall to find Lynette the *perfect* gift and was trying to get me to tell him what kind of flowers girls like. I tell you he's smitten." Alex swung his leg over the stool next to the chessboard. "I stopped by B. Dalton's to check out that new book by Stephen Hawking that James told me about. Plus, I found a book Michelle's been looking for. Okay, light or dark?"

"No thanks, Alex. I'll pass on the chess, thanks." I frowned down at the beautifully carved wooden chess pieces from the set Uncle Bartho had found in Naples. This time I did not stop to strategize or contemplate a potential move. "True gratitude," I mumbled. "James stood me up."

"Oh, come on, Jana."

I had to will myself not to cry. It was true. James had stood me up. *Give a person some looks and a little prestige and it goes straight to his head,* I distinctly remember thinking.

— ᴏᴂ —

It was at around seven, while I was in my room supposedly reading *The Iliad* but really just skimming over the words, when the doorbell finally rang. I lifted my head and stared toward the inside of my slightly open bedroom door. After a few seconds I could hear muffled voices. "Jana?" my brother finally called. "James is here."

Pulling in my breath, I jerked my head away from the door, turned back to the wall, then looked back at the inside of the bedroom door once again. I didn't answer.

A few seconds later I heard Alex taking the stairs two, possibly three, at a time. "James is here," he said, tapping. "You decent?"

"Tell him I'm awfully busy," I said.

"Jana, come on," Alex said. "This is James."

I didn't answer.

"Fine, suit yourself." Alex started back down the stairs and when I heard him hit the ground floor with his normal thud, I pulled myself to a sitting position. I waited a few seconds longer, then, with narrowed eyes, slid my legs off the bed and onto the hardwood floor.

Chapter Twenty-Five

ᴥ

Well, hello James. Is that how I should say it when I see him when he gets off the plane? Or should I just be casual? *Oh, hi, James, you're back.* No, that sounds insipid.

If Cassie were here at the airport, I know how she'd greet James. She'd *rock* the place with unabashed *exuberance.* She'd race over and envelop James with her classic bear hug, all the while shouting out her trademark salutation. Or maybe that salutation has changed now. Maybe instead of "Wowsers!" she'd be bellowing "Aloha!" now.

Cassie flew to Hawaii a few months ago and was hired at the Polynesian Cultural Center where she demonstrates, yes, the hula. She says that despite the fact that she still has a good bushel basket of weight to lose, they like her attitude there. "I think they figure that my being willing to make a fool of myself will encourage others who aren't the perfect ten to go for it as well," she wrote in her last e-mail. "You know—if I can do it, anybody can!"

Even though Cassie's not here, there are plenty of others who look just as ready to pounce on James. Why am I worrying about how I'll greet James when Ruby and Topaz Backus, prepared and organized as always, arrived about fifteen minutes ago with hundreds of balloons and a banner that reads: "Welcome Home, Super-Jim." Butch, who's a yell-leader at Ohio State now, has been practicing an actual welcome home cheer with Emily Fitzmeier who just swooped by me about five minutes ago. If I hadn't immediately lifted the *Time* magazine I'd just picked up, I'm sure she would have seen me. Oh yes, it's obvious James will be getting quite the reception.

It wasn't with balloons or banners or a bear hug that I greeted James that Saturday of our senior year after he'd kept me waiting for over four hours. I'm afraid I wouldn't have done anything resembling a toe touch even if I'd been capable. I didn't even give James a low five, not to mention a high one. I wasn't about to let anyone get away with treating me like some kind of a discard.

"Nice of you to finally show!" I said when I located James and Alex in the family room. "I waited for you. In fact, I waited and waited! But you didn't even have the decency to call."

"The fact is—"

"The fact is that you're a *somebody* now, isn't it?" I interrupted. "The fact is that you're *important*. You're *wonderful*! You've made more prestigious friends this past year. And who needs the *old* friends after you used them to become president of Fairport! Isn't that the fact, James?"

"Jana, get a grip!" Alex's light brown eyes had turned into ping-pong balls. "Sorry about this, James. She's completely lost it."

"Jana, I wanted to—" James was still trying to explain.

"I single-handedly turned you from a complete geekkenstein into a VIP," I interrupted again, "but *you*—you have no gratitude!"

"A geekken-what?" asked Alex, raising his eyebrows as high as they'd go.

"If you'd give me a chance to—" James had pushed his glasses against the bridge of his nose three times in a row and was inching toward the French doors that led to our patio, undoubtedly wishing he were outside of them.

"Yes, please, go ahead and explain if you can, James," I continued, following him. "But first I have a question: Is this what your religion that you're always trying to share, teaches you? Is this how the Book of Mormon you and Alex have been wanting me to read instructs you to treat people? Does your church teach you to dump your old friends after you've used them to get what you want? Is that what your *Holy Ghost* tells you to do?" The instant I'd spit out the words I was sorry and I cleared my throat nervously. I'd once again gone too far, and I knew it. Unfortunately once words are out, you can't rein them back in.

Both Alex and James were staring at me. Alex came to first. "Man, Jana," he breathed.

James stopped moving backward. He lowered his eyes and peered down at the floor, his mouth puckered. Finally he lifted his head, took off his glasses and slipped them into his shirt pocket. Little flares had formed in his light blue eyes. "Thanks for stopping to breathe," he said quietly. "May I have a turn to talk now?"

"By all means. Be my guest."

Alex backed to the couch and then pushed himself into the corner, pulling the cushion toward him.

"Go right ahead," I continued, lifting my hand at our friend.

"Thank you." James paused and then started to speak in a low, controlled voice. "The truth is, Jana, that Dolly had been wanting to tour our historical church site at Kirtland and she couldn't go the last time Alex and I took a group."

Alex pulled the cushion down, ready to add I was sure, how "awesome" that site was. I'd heard much more than I'd cared to hear about it. When I glared at him, my brother lifted his hand with a "What?" expression.

"This morning was the only time we could go," James continued, "and I let Dolly know that I needed to leave early enough to be back in time for my chess game with you. But when I got to her house she said that Shereen Quinn really wanted to come along but was registering for some kind of a beauty pageant and was running late and asked if we could pick her up there."

"Oh, well, my goodness, you poor—"

James raised his hand. "I'm not finished."

"He's not finished," repeated my brother.

"When we got to Kirtland, there was an electrical outage of some kind in the visitor's center, more than likely because of the weather, and the tour was delayed. We caught a later tour, but afterward, the power company's truck was blocking our car and it took us a while to find the driver. It was pelting rain by then— really coming down. As soon as we got on the interstate, we realized that we should have taken a side route because a semi had rolled over and cars were lined up for miles. It took us about two hours to move what seemed like ten miles. Dolly's cell had run out of power, Shereen's wouldn't connect for some reason, and I'd forgotten mine. Luckily, the time wasn't wasted. It turned out the girls had quite a few questions about what we'd seen and heard on the tour and while we were stuck in traffic, I answered them the best that I could. Now that's the truth."

"Right. And next you'll be telling me that you prayed right there on the interstate. That you got out and knelt by the side of the car—you and Dolly and Shereen and whoever else!" *The most beautiful girls in the school,* I was thinking.

"No, but we did pray inside the car."

"Oh, I see. I'm supposed to believe that you spent almost this entire day talking religion—even praying!—with Dolly Devonshire and her friends. Is that what you're telling me?"

"Pretty much."

The trouble was I *did* believe him. Furthermore, this information, I realized, should actually have made me feel worse not better. I hadn't heard any more about Dolly and Shereen still studying the LDS faith and I'd assumed that they'd lost interest and had moved on.

I could tell James was extremely frustrated with me. "At least *some* people are openhearted enough to be willing to listen," he said, his voice raspy. "I invited you to go to Kirtland with us the last few times that Alex and I went, remember?"

"I had other plans," I said, folding my arms.

"All four times?"

"I'm a very busy girl."

James was quiet for several seconds, his head bouncing

slightly. "You know, just a minute ago, you insinuated that you single-handedly changed me last year. The truth is you had *some* help and cooperation."

"That's right," said Alex, lowering the cushion again. "Hey, I gave you the shirts off my back, Buddy." It was obvious Alex was trying to lighten things up, but James and I ignored him completely.

"I was open to your ideas, Jana," said James. "I was *reachable*—which is more than I can say for you."

"What do you . . . what . . ."

"What could *you* possibly have to improve? I just might have a few tips. In fact, why don't you step closer to the mirror."

Alex readjusted the cushion and tucked himself even deeper into the end of the couch. I felt like asking him if he wanted some popcorn.

"Oh, I get it. I know what you're doing," I said to James as I backed toward our wrought iron, framed mirror over the stone fireplace. "Now it's my turn, is that it?"

"Well, *I* was able to handle it when you critiqued me pretty thoroughly last year, remember?"

"Fine!" I turned and faced the mirror, unwilling to admit I was a little curious to hear what he'd have to say.

"What do you see, Jana?" asked James quietly.

"I don't know, just . . . I don't know." I didn't especially want to look at myself right then and I pulled my gaze from my reflection and glanced around the room. I narrowed my eyes when I got to my brother who appeared to be feeling a little too comfortable. I finally looked back into the mirror.

"I'll tell you what I see," said James. "I see an eighteen-year-old girl whose highlighted, golden-brown hair is styled exactly right and whose makeup is just about perfect. I see someone who exercises and keeps herself up and stands up straight and wears the right clothes that are the right size with colors that emphasize her green eyes with blue flecks or blue eyes with green flecks, depending on whether she's wearing blue or green."

I hadn't blushed in years, but I could feel my face heating up like a candelabra. In the mirror, the follow-up telltale light crimson crept into my cheeks. "But how you look *at* people is important, too, Jana." James obviously remembered what I'd said to him all those months ago when I'd had *him* facing the mirror. "Now it happens that you look at people with your chin too high and your nose in the air as if you're saying, 'I'm better than you are, World, and I know everything there is to know!'"

I objected. "What are you talking about?" He was describing our old enemy Lyla Fannen and some of her former friends, but not me. "That's not true. I—" Only then I noticed that my chin was lifted at that very moment and I pulled back in surprise and lowered it.

"It's not easy to see yourself in action, after all. We could follow you around with a camera, but even if we did, you probably still wouldn't see yourself clearly. It's true, you're book smart, and you're definitely street smart, but nobody knows everything, Jana. The sad part is you don't even know the basics," he paused, "because you won't—"

James stopped talking. He struggled with the words, opened his mouth, and then shut it again. Beads of perspiration were perched on his forehead like tiny birds on a power line. "You know what, I've gotta go," he said. "I'm angry and I've said too much already. I need to leave right now." He backed toward the French doors, turned, jerked one side open, and hurried out.

"I won't what?" I asked, following him out the open door. "Study your church? You're talking about your church literature, aren't you?" I called after him. "Is *that* how your church's leaders recommend you offer it to people?"

He peered back at me over his glasses, his face unreadable, and shaking as he headed toward our side gate. I was shaking myself.

"Whoooeee, I've never seen James that upset!" said my brother.

I flipped around. "Alex, do you think I'm a stubborn, snooty, know-it-all who's completely lacking in humility? that I'm a headstrong brat?"

Alex shrugged. "Why are you acting like this is new information?"

"You *agree* with James's assessment of me?"

Alex nodded. "Oh, yeah. Absolutely."

"James has some nerve saying those things when there's no way he'd be where he is right now if I hadn't worked and sacrificed with everything I had to help him get elected last year. And then he says *I* don't know the basics? He's the one who doesn't know the basics! He didn't even know how to comb his hair before he met me."

"I imagine the *basics* he was talking about just might be more important basics such as where we come from and where we're going—those kind of basics," said Alex in what I felt was a pious manner. "And um, I'm not talking about Chicago," he added, raising his eyebrows.

"Right. That's exactly what I thought," I said, slapping hard at a pillow. "He's upset because I haven't read your Mormon literature. Well, you know what? If I read every church's literature, I'd be reading from now until 5000 A.D. Am I going to investigate everything? Do I need to investigate the Amish church and the Jehovah's Witnesses and the Shakers and Quakers and hey, maybe that zealot James told you about who lived at the top of a pole for thirty-seven years even started a religion! I'll have to investigate that!"

I plopped down on the couch and this time *I* pulled the cushion up under my eyes. Then I pulled it back down and flipped it behind me. With a lunge, I popped back up and started pacing the floor. "Look, what I've tried and tried to tell you and James and Mom and Ruthie and Phil and even Cassie is that I'm just not religious. Why should I read your Mormon Church information when I'm just not religious?"

"It wouldn't hurt you to just look at it. That's all anybody's asking, Jana."

"I have!"

"You have?"

"Yes! I opened the Book of Mormon and looked at it for a few seconds once, but that was enough."

"Oh, so a few seconds was enough?"

"Please leave me alone!" I headed for the stairs to my room, wishing I'd never come down. I had the feeling James and Alex were wishing the same thing.

"Maybe reading some religious literature would help you with your attitude problem!" Alex called up after me. "I've said it before and I'll say it again: You have a *major* attitude problem!"

"Unmitigated moron," I muttered. "No—*Mormon*. Same thing. *Imbécile!*" I muttered in French.

Chapter Twenty-Six

I t was quiet in the house. Mom had gone to bed right after she'd returned from her "nice affair," happily exhausted. About an hour and a half before, I'd heard Alex leave to pick up Michelle from work. For the last hour or so I'd been lying on my bed staring at the ceiling. Now I got up, limped to my dresser, and looked into the alabaster-framed mirror above it. I lifted my chin and lowered it. Was it true what James had said? Was I a know-it-all brat?

I didn't feel that way inside. I didn't *feel* I knew everything. Apparently even my own twin brother agreed with James's assessment of me. *Well good*, I remember thinking. *Let everybody believe I'm confident and in control.* It was what I'd been trying to believe myself. Apparently the "act as if" principle was working. "If you're not feeling confident, *act* as if you are!" Dr. Griffin had shared that principle with me in one of my therapy sessions. It was a bit pop-psych for a professional, but it seemed to work.

Okay, maybe I overdid it a little. Maybe I was the one who was the big fake. But there was no denying I was smart. I was definitely smart. You bet I was smart! I lifted my chin and this time did not lower it. I not only had a chance at winning the Ohio State Chess Championship, but I'd just been accepted to Harvard! I'd soon be attending a prestigious Ivy League school, and James had the nerve to tell *me* I didn't know the basics?

Maybe he was right and I didn't know exactly who I was and where I came from, but who did? Who did know the basics? Who knew anything for sure? Religions claimed they had the answers, but they didn't. If they did, why would they all differ in their beliefs and opinions on various subjects?

The Mormons believed a baptism was null and void should your toe not be immersed with the rest of you. Faithful Catholics just sprinkled a few drops on your head and called it good. Still they both insisted they were performing this ordinance or ritual the correct way.

And faith was nothing more than conjecture with a little emotion poured in! Not even the scientific experts knew for certain where we came from and where we are going! It was *all* just conjecture! But fine! If Alex and James—and Mom too, for that matter—wanted me to read the material that badly, I'd look at it. Hey, I'd taken speed-reading! I could read and refute this fluff in a matter of minutes!

I was pretty sure that Alex still studied LDS material on a daily basis, so I took large angry steps down the hall to his room. I located some pamphlets in his bookcase along with a book James had recommended more than once: *A Marvelous Work and a Wonder.* I slipped the pamphlets inside the book and hurried to my bedroom where I began flipping through the pages. Finally I slowed down and read more carefully.

The church Christ established when he lived on the earth, one particular pamphlet claimed, had disappeared from the earth. It explained that the apostles died one by one, and then gradually Christian doctrine was revamped by people who weren't even Christians. I had to admit that the pamphlet presented a good argument for what it referred to as "the Great Apostasy."

But wasn't the Mormon Church cutting off its own golden foot by claiming that Christ's church had disappeared from the earth? Mormons did, after all, profess to be Christians, didn't they? I read on. The Church of Jesus Christ of Latter-day Saints, I read, claimed that the authority to act in God's name was restored to the earth. The priesthood, according to this pamphlet, had been reinstated by heavenly messengers. Well that was bold! But there was even more.

The pamphlet said that the newly restored church was the *same* church Christ established when he was on the earth. So that explained the term "latter-day." I raised my eyebrows. Beyond bold! But so what? Why should any of this matter to me? I didn't even believe in a god.

There was another pamphlet about the Book of Mormon, and I picked that up next and began to read. Apparently the Book of Mormon was not some kind of a Mormon Bible as I'd assumed. The pamphlet explained that it was actually *additional* scripture. This, I had to admit, was news to me.

Curious now, I tiptoed downstairs to see if a copy of the Book of Mormon was still on the coffee table where Mom or Alex had left it. I suspected they kept a copy there for this exact purpose—so that I'd pick it up. Well, I'd thrill them for once. I took the copy up to my room and turned a few pages to a section called I Nephi.

I hadn't read far when I came to a dream somebody named Lehi, the narrator's father, had had. When I reached the part about a tall building, I was again stunned. *I'd* dreamed this dream! Okay, maybe it hadn't been this *exact* dream, but it was eerily similar. It was one of those dreams you don't easily forget and I could still remember that there was a building from which Lyla Fannen and her friends were making fun of those down below. My dream hadn't had a rod in it or a tree—but there'd been a path that had turned into a football field. And my dream had had tortillas and soda and potatoes in it, not spiritual fruit, but other than that . . .

When I heard Alex pulling in the driveway, I slipped the Book of Mormon and the other materials under my goose-down pillow and grabbed Dickens's *Great Expectations*.

Alex unlocked the door downstairs and I heard him coming up the stairs. Would he knock? He did. "Wuzz up?"

"Nothing much. Did you have a good time?"

"We did. You should have come." My brother stepped into my room, pulled my vanity stool toward him, straddled it, and proceeded to relate how he and Michelle, Robbie, Butch Torkinson, Lynette Trist, Celia Pinnock, and Paul had all played *Cranium* and that Celia had done an amazing impression of Barbra Streisand. "Butch is better at trivia than I thought he'd be," my brother said with respect in his voice. "He knew it was Doc Holliday who fought alongside the Earp brothers at the OK Corral." My brother was presenting me with much greater detail concerning his evening than usual, no doubt trying to make up for shouting at me earlier about my attitude. "And Michelle's a good artist," he added with a lilt of pride in his voice.

"She's smart as well."

Alex nodded with enthusiasm. "That too. She's definitely smart."

We'd had these joint Michelle-appreciation sessions before and it was obvious my brother was as smitten with Michelle as he'd claimed Butch was with Lynette—maybe more so. At last he stood, stretched his legs, and said good night.

A few seconds later I heard him turn on the tap in the bathroom. I guessed he was filling the water container for the leopard geckos he'd adopted from the young son of one of my mother's "sisters" in the ward. In a few seconds Alex would be feeding his hamsters and his tropical fish and the wounded finch he'd found outside by the forsythia. Then he'd be praying.

I held my breath wondering if he would notice the missing literature. But soon the hall darkened and I knew that he had shut off his light. When it remained quiet, I eagerly, but quietly, pulled the Book of Mormon out from under my pillow, flipped through a few pages, and read through this Lehi's dream one more time. Again, it seemed like such an odd coincidence that *my* dream had been so similar to this Book of Mormon character's.

After finishing the chapter, I continued thumbing through the pages, stopping here and there to read more closely. At around two A.M. I finally fell asleep.

Chapter Twenty-Seven

ᵒᶜ⊃

When the doorbell rang that next day, a Sunday, Mom and Alex were still at church. Grace, my mother had discovered, was between apartments and needed a place to stay the night before. She was in the kitchen, putting the finishing touches on some kind of a Greek dish for dinner. That left me to check the peephole. James was standing on our front porch in his Sunday clothes, looking so forlorn and upset that I went ahead and answered the door in my bright purple bathrobe and Mickey Mouse slippers. "Hi."

"I just heard you got accepted to Harvard," he said quietly.

"I did."

"It was probably something you wanted to celebrate yesterday, wasn't it?"

I bobbled my head. "Well, yes, sort of. Come in." I led him to the living room, my slippers flopping, then lowered my less-than-elegant self to the cream couch, highly aware that I hadn't even run a comb through my hair.

James didn't seem to notice how bedraggled I looked as he sat down across from me. "Look, I came over to apologize. Getting into Harvard is an amazing accomplishment and it should have been a great day for you. But instead you had to wait for me for hours. I wish I'd had some control over that, but I honestly didn't. What I did have control over is how I acted last night and what I said." Genuine misery permeated his voice. "I made it sound like I didn't appreciate what you did for me last year and that's not the case at all. You . . . I . . . ."

He ran his hand through the new closer-cropped cut that was perfect for his hair's coarse texture. "I recognize full well how much you helped me and that it was because of you I ended up having the chance to be president of Fairport this past year. There's no way I could have pulled off what I did without you. I had no business making it sound otherwise. You're the man, as Alex would say." He laughed softly. "I mean the wo*man*. And you were right that our Church leaders wouldn't recommend we attempt to spread doctrine through shame and insult. I can't believe I was so critical and plowed into you like that." James flicked a glance at me and half-smiled in embarrassment.

"I finally read some of the LDS literature you and Alex and everybody else have been wanting me to read," I heard myself say. "In fact, I read until really late."

"You did?" James looked at me as though I'd turned into an alien in pink tights and a tutu.

"Yes, and I have to say it made a lot more sense than I expected it to."

"I've tried to tell you that." As he leaned forward anxiously, I noticed how nicely his white shirt was starched and that the stripe in his blue tie matched his eyes perfectly. "We've *all* been trying to tell you that."

I raised my hand, spreading my fingers. "Yes, well, don't get excited. I'm not saying that *I* believe it, but . . . well, I'll admit this: I can see now how a normal and intelligent person *could* believe it—*if* that person bought into the concept of angelic messengers and the supernatural, of course. That's a nice suit, by the way. It has a nice clean cut to it." It *was* a good-looking suit—kind of a deep gray, and it fit James beautifully.

"Thanks. I found it where you and Alex suggested—The Gentlemen's Closet. You were right. They really helped me with the fit, and the price wasn't bad either." He paused. "You know why I need this suit, right?"

"Your mission." I said it with a sigh in my voice. James would turn nineteen at the end of the summer. I'd been aware for some time that a mission for a practicing nineteen-year-old male in the LDS Church is almost as much a rite of passage as bar mitzvah is for a Jewish thirteen-year-old male.

"I'm working on my papers and plan to turn them in as soon as it's allowed—sometime around the end of May."

"*Papers?*"

"They're kind of an application."

"Ah." I nodded my head. It wasn't unusual for James to be ahead of schedule and have everything carefully planned out. It was one of the reasons he'd made such an excellent school president. "You know, you've kept up your appearance really well, James. In fact, you're looking better than ever."

"Compliments of Jana Bennings," he said.

"Okay, I *will* take some of the credit there. But the character part? Compliments of your Church, right? And your parents, and your training, and maybe even good genes." James's integrity intrigued me even more than his intellect, and this rare commodity had become the thing I admired most about him.

"It sounds trite to say this because you hear it a lot from members, especially in the fast and testimony meeting our church holds at the beginning of each month, but I honestly *don't* know where I'd be if I hadn't had this church and this gospel in my life. Maybe I'd have twenty-three piercings like Garlia," he said.

"Twenty. She's cut back."

"Okay, twenty. And maybe I'd smoke and drink. Or maybe I'd be addicted to drugs and have to get help in some rehab program in Florida." *Like Lyla Fannen*, we both thought, but didn't say.

"Or wear your hair like Garlia's friend." I snorted a little as I pictured James in an overgrown multi-colored Mohawk.

James remained serious. "Seriously, Jana, I honestly don't know who or where I'd be without the gospel of Jesus Christ in my life."

"Sorry, James, but I can't even imagine you with piercings. Okay, possibly a tattoo—one that reads 'Choose the Right.'"

"In the middle of my forehead, right?"

"Exactly."

James smiled a little now and shook his head at the rug.

I tapped my foot, wrinkled my nose, and took a deep breath. "I do have a few questions I thought maybe you could answer for me."

He looked up. "About our church?"

"Yes, about the Mormon faith. Let me get them." I stood up self-consciously and flapped my slippers into the study where I'd left the legal pad on the armrest of the leather chair. I definitely had a few questions—about three sheets full. Some were questions that were probably fairly common but that I'd never heard properly answered.

How much of the Old Testament did the Church of Jesus Christ believe should be taken literally and how much symbolically? What about polygamy? Then there were questions about specifics I'd just barely read: If this God of the Book of Mormon was the same God as the New Testament, why would he have had this character named Nephi kill a man and break a commandment He'd set up himself? I'd also included some of the same old science versus religion concerns: Where did the Mormons theorize dinosaurs fit into the picture? Yes, James had said the *days* spoken of in the Bible could have been six long periods of time, but exactly how long were these periods of time?

And I had some specific questions about the pamphlet called *The Plan of Salvation.* I was anxious to find out what made a person eligible to be in the Mormon version of heaven and more about this spirit world where those who had passed on were apparently to go—yes, I wanted to know where the Mormons felt Uncle Bartho was.

"You really do have a few questions," James said as he surveyed the list.

"You know me—always thirsting for answers." I pressed my fingers hard against my cheekbone, then flipped my index finger forward. "Just please keep in mind that I'm only curious and this doesn't mean that much. In fact, I'd appreciate it if you wouldn't mention any of this to Alex or my mother. They'd just get excited and there's nothing whatsoever to get excited about."

I glanced toward the kitchen and began speaking more quietly, paranoid that Grace might overhear and tell Mom. It was vitally important that James keep the fact that I was seeking answers about the Mormon faith just between us *and* that he not get excited himself. Yes, I was fascinated with what I'd read, but I *was* just curious and he needed to know that that was where it ended.

"Just look at this as a good exercise into what you might face on your mission. It'll be good practice for you."

"It sure looks that way," James said, laughing nervously as he continued to survey the questions. "In fact, it looks like I'm going to need to do some research."

"Only if you have the time." I knew he would be extremely busy during the remaining few weeks of school. "There's no rush. I can wait."

"I'll make the time."

And that's exactly what James did. In spite of the fact that we were in the middle of school elections again and that the following weeks were bursting with activities requiring his superhuman attention, James made the time to search out answers for me. He brought me additional pamphlets and books, including the science and religion publication he'd told me about the year before. I studied it, and everything else he brought me, carefully, and again had to admit I saw much greater merit in what I was reading than I would ever have dreamed.

— ⚬∂ —

The next few weeks passed by faster than yes, a speeding bullet, and within what seemed like seconds, the final elections were over. One day there he was, Alex's and my best friend, up on the stage saying good-bye to the students of Fairport High. It had been a phenomenal year and I don't think there was a single student who did not stand to applaud and cheer.

By the time James finally had a chance to speak, he couldn't. Instead, he pointed at the other officers on the stand, and then at those who had supported him, including members of our old committee who'd helped him get elected in the first place: Cassie, Bud, Sadie, Sergei, to name a few, and of course, Alex . . . and then me. Yes, he nodded right at me.

Then, tears falling, he fanned his arm across the rest of the audience to include everybody there. "I couldn't have done it alone," he said, lifting his hand ceiling-ward. Everyone in the audience knew who he was including then. "We . . . we . . . did . . . it to . . . gether!" This time the students of Fairport High remained silent, some with their heads bowed, some with their heads lifted, most of them crying softly or sniffing.

It wasn't until a few minutes later, as each of the old officers stood to announce his or her replacement and James introduced, to nobody's surprise, Topaz Backus as Fairport's new student body president, that it struck me full force. Our reign was over. I looked around for Alex and found him a few rows back with Butch, Bud, and Terrance. When our eyes met, he nodded at me in understanding, and ran his index finger across his bottom lid. I blinked back at him, returning his nod, my lips pulled together tightly, then looked back up at James.

How I was able to control my emotions, I'm not sure. But somehow I managed to keep it together during the remainder of the school day. But that afternoon, I sobbed my way home. As I passed the football field, the marquee, the old tree—all the familiar sights—I knew for a surety that I would never forget our senior year, thanks to a president who had done exactly what he'd said he would: lifted us to heights we didn't know we could reach. It'd been a miraculous year, a truly *super* year. James had made an unbelievably good president and he really was an incredible person, a real live superman. Of all the people I'd ever met, he was one of the greatest—maybe even *the* greatest. I knew it the moment he stood on that stage and gave the credit to everyone else. As soon as I got home I hurried straight to my room and read until I'd completed the Book of Mormon.

— ᎧᎧ —

Early the next morning, my friend surprised me at 8 o'clock sharp. Again I greeted him in my less than glamorous purple robe. "If you've got your chess tournament in a couple of days," James said, "we'd better get busy."

"You're something, James Orville," I responded, still drowsy from reading until late, but genuinely touched.

All that weekend, in between school functions and his church meetings and responsibilities, James and I played chess. Still, as I walked into the library at Cleveland State to start my first match at the advanced level, I was highly aware that I wasn't nearly as focused and prepared as I needed to be. I lasted that round and several more and even a full round longer than the year before, but then I found myself thoroughly outplayed by Nataliya Vinogradova, an amazing strategist, who, like Sergei, had immigrated from Moscow a few years before. I suspected she'd read the chess bible backwards and forwards, and had possibly even contributed to it.

"I lost again," I told James and Alex.

"You lost first place," James clarified. "But what about all the times you won? You're one of the top ten players in state!" James grinned. "That's nothing to thumb your nose at!"

"Only first place is good enough," I stated.

Alex rolled his eyes and shook his head at James as if to say, *That's Jana.*

Once again, however, I wasn't nearly as devastated as I'd anticipated. If someone had told me even two months earlier that I would take a loss in the state chess tournament on my last chance to take first place with so little grief, I would have told that someone he'd lost his marbles and was operating on peanut shells.

And if that same someone had told me I would be as intense as I'd been about pursuing information about any religion, but especially the Mormon religion, I would have wondered if that person had just arrived on earth from the planet Whackonia.

Much had changed.

I had changed.

Chapter Twenty-Eight

T he day after our tenure at Fairport was officially over and
we'd walked across the football field in our graduation
gowns and received the special honors we'd earned—in my
case, a top 5% academic cord among others—I actually agreed to
allow James to make an appointment for me with some Mormon
missionaries he said were officially called to answer doctrinal questions such as mine.

"I can't keep up with you," he said.

The missionaries—who surprised me by being girls—presented
a series of lessons with information that, frankly, I'd already studied. The lessons did give me a good overview, however, and helped
me see more clearly how everything fit together.

"So what about this historic Kirtland?" I finally asked James.

"You want to go?"

"Well, I *would* like to see if it's as amazing as my brother seems
to think it is."

When James tried to disguise his laugh of excitement with a cough, I found myself hiding a smile.

The following Saturday, James and I—and *Alex*—were traveling to Kirtland. It was impossible to keep secrets from my brother for long and he had caught wind of our plans and insisted on coming along. I suspect that he'd known for some time I was taking the lessons from the missionaries and had been waiting for me to tell him.

Soon we were touring a small white temple which, because the main faction of the church had had to leave the area rather quickly, was owned by an offshoot of a Mormon group. The guide mentioned many evangelical occurrences which James explained were part of the restoration of all things. In another section of Kirtland, not far from the temple, we toured six buildings, including a mill, a schoolhouse, and a store which had been restored and rebuilt to look as authentic as the original buildings.

I listened carefully to the descriptions of what took place in these buildings, especially about what had transpired upstairs in the Newel K. Whitney store. When, as a sidelight, the guide showed how Mrs. Whitney had baked bread in her state-of-the-art hole next to the fireplace and had the challenge of making sure her full-length skirts didn't catch fire, I thanked the stars that I'd been born in an era of Levis and microwaves.

Next we drove right into the center of Amish territory to what was called the John Johnson farm where Joseph and Emma Smith had apparently stayed for a period of time and where Joseph had done a great deal of "inspired" work. I had to admit that I definitely felt something when the guide, an older woman dressed in pioneer attire, showed us the bedroom where Joseph and his family had been staying when a mob attacked. The Smiths' young twins had been ill with measles when the men burst in, and one of the twins had died a short time later.

Yes, I felt something. But then again who wouldn't have? This man, Joseph Smith, had not led an easy life and neither had his wife or children. He'd sacrificed a great deal for the visions he believed he'd had. I found myself wondering about the twin who had survived and how she'd coped in life without her brother.

"What did you think?" James asked on the way home.

"I think I have quite a bit more reading to do," I answered.

He and Alex glanced at each other and had I not been there would probably have given each other high fives.

— ᴏᴆ —

The next few nights, I devoured the additional books I'd learned about on the tour: the Doctrine and Covenants and the Pearl of Great Price. But two days later, when the missionaries tried once again to commit me to baptism, I balked.

"I'm not ready," I said. "I still don't know enough."

"I honestly think you know as much if not more than we do," Sister Fitzgerald responded with a smile. "I've never met an investigator who knows as much as you've learned in such a short time."

"Well, I don't *feel* like I know enough."

Sister Fitzgerald tapped her scriptures, her lips pursed. "I'm thinking there might be something specific you're allowing to hold you back," she finally said. She paused for several more seconds.

"It could be something you're not even consciously aware of your-self. But I think we need to find out what it might be because it's hard to deal with an issue if it isn't identified."

I stared at her, hypnotized.

"Try to determine during these next couple of days what it might be that's keeping you from making the progress you need to make—whether it's a particular commandment or point of doctrine—then when it's out in the open, maybe we can help you deal with it."

I nodded slowly. "Okay. I'll think about it."

I drove home in stunned silence, climbed the stairs to my room, and sat down at my desk. Then I laid my head on my hands because I didn't need to think about it. I already knew what was wrong.

Even after all this time and study, it boiled down to the same basic problem—messages from heaven. The LDS Church's entire premise was based on faith in such heavenly manifestations.

So why, I wondered, had I allowed it to go this far? I blinked, sat up, and buried my face in my hands as that answer came to me as well. It was actually quite pitiful, really. I was no different than anybody else. I was aching for some structure, some answers, *some-thing* to cling to like that rod in Lehi's dream. I hoped to taste the white fruit on the tree. I wanted what seemed to be making my family so happy. I wanted to complete the picture and be unified with the people I loved most: Alex and Mom, Aunt Ruthie and Phillip, and yes, even my good friend James. I wanted the very things I'd judged others for wanting. I huffed out a sob. But the desire to be a part of something and to join in with the people I loved, even the urgency to have some guidance, didn't seem like adequate reasons to commit to a religion, even a good religion.

— ♋ —

I broke the news to James and Alex and the missionaries that Wednesday. "I'll be completely truthful with you," I said quietly. "I admire the Mormon Church and its people and even its principles and doctrines and that's something I didn't think I'd ever hear myself say. Of all the Christian churches, the Mormon faith presents the most powerful argument. But"—James looked up as Alex looked down—"For me, there's just too broad a gap between what the academic community teaches and what religions teach. I've talked about that with James. But I'm still just not seeing how the two viewpoints could ever come together. I've read what you've given me, but there are just too many unanswered questions. I'd like to believe in God, I really would, but I don't know that such a belief would be justified."

The silence was thick as my brother and James and the missionaries tried to absorb what I'd just said. I deemed it a good thing Mom wasn't there; I'd sworn Alex, James, and Mary Jane to secrecy in this instance. My mother, I knew, would be blubbering like a baby at this moment and it was difficult enough disappointing my brother, James, and these missionaries I'd come to respect.

"Why do you always make everything so complicated? It doesn't need to be complicated!" I wasn't surprised to hear Alex blurt this out. I knew what he'd say next as well. "As soon as I read the Book of Mormon—*zowie*—I knew it was true." He placed his hand against the left side of his chest.

"Zowie? Wowsers! Now you're sounding like Cassie," I reacted. "Well, I'm sorry, but that didn't happen to me, Alex. I guess I'm not a *zowie* kind of person."

"Testimonies develop in different ways," explained Sister Fitzgerald calmly. "Not everybody has a *zowie* or *wowsers* experience. For most people, a testimony comes far more gradually."

"Line upon line," added orange-headed Sister Spires, a former waitress from Arkansas.

Sister Fitzgerald continued, "You're right about the fact that not all questions have been answered. Even though there have been a great many things revealed, there are still many things that haven't been fully explained to us. I've come to the conclusion that we can't know everything because at this point our minds aren't advanced enough. It'd be like teaching calculus to a two-year-old."

I'd heard that from James once before too.

Sister Spires picked up the thread. "Now this may sound like a backwards approach, but by finding out if the Book of Mormon really was translated by inspiration and that Joseph Smith really was a prophet, you can find out that there is a God—even without knowing the answer to every question."

It sounded simple in a way, but in another way—simplistic. "And how would you suggest I do that?"

"Just continue studying and praying."

"That's all?" I was disappointed.

"That's it. Well, that and coming to church." Sister Fitzgerald looked more like she was fifteen instead of twenty-one or twenty-two, and it still fascinated me that a soft voice could have such command. "Do you remember the promise that Moroni makes at the end of the Book of Mormon?" she asked me then.

Sister Spires whipped me her open copy of the Book of Mormon. "Right here," she said.

I took the book. "Yes, I remember that."

"Would you mind reading the promise in the last part of the verse again?" asked Sister Fitzgerald.

I didn't particularly feel I needed to read it again, but decided that it wouldn't hurt me to cooperate this one last time. "Okay." I took a deep breath and read: "'And if ye shall ask with a sincere heart, with real intent, having faith in Christ, he will manifest the truth of it unto you, by the power of the Holy Ghost. And by the power of the Holy Ghost ye may know the truth of all things.'"

"So what does that tell us we'll learn if we pray with faith and real intent?" Sister Fitzgerald asked softly.

"The truth of all things," I said.

"And by whose power?"

"The power of the Holy Ghost."

"That's right. You can learn the truth of *all* things if you pray with real intent, with faith in Christ."

"But that's the catch-22 about all this: How can I pray with faith in Christ if I don't really have faith in Christ? How do you ask God if you don't know if He's there? That's like talking on the phone when you don't know if anyone's on the other end."

"Yes, but when you're not sure if someone's on the other end of the line, don't you keep talking until you *make* sure?" asked Sister Fitzgerald.

I sighed and bobbled my head from side to side because it was a good point.

"Your brother's right," Sister Spires chimed in. "It doesn't need to be complicated. If you pray with real intent, the Spirit will manifest the truth, just like the scripture says. You'll feel it."

"It happened to me," said James quietly. "I received that witness."

I turned to him slowly. "You really did?"

"I did. And the Spirit still helps me in my everyday decisions. If there weren't a god, why would we feel so much better when we do things that are good than when we do things that aren't? Why would human beings have a conscience?"

Again a good point. The missionaries agreed and added their testimonies as well. Alex repeated his strong confirmation of the truthfulness of the Mormon Church.

"Okay," I said. What else could I do? "I'll try once more." When Alex made a "yes" fist, I smiled at him sadly. I managed to lift one corner of my mouth at James, who was nodding slowly. *Just don't expect too much, my friends,* I thought.

— ᖚᘓ —

In spite of my misgivings, that night I began reading the Book of Mormon for the second time. This time I read much more slowly than I had before and this time I read very carefully. When I came to Lehi's dream again, I thought for a few seconds that I actually felt something—a strange swelling sensation. But once again I tabbed it as an emotional reaction. Whether the account of Lehi's dream, and the whole book for that matter, was fiction or nonfiction, it touched me deeply that Lehi wanted to share the sweet, delicious fruit on the tree with his family members—even Laman and Lemuel who weren't particularly lovable, obedient sons.

Laman and Lemuel did not comply with their father's urgings in the dream anymore than they'd followed his counsel and guidance otherwise. The two had been upset from the beginning of the story that their father had forced his family to flee from their home in Jerusalem. And who could blame them, really?

I sunk down a little into the leather chair. I could completely relate to their resentment at having to leave their home and their fine things, possibly their servants, their wealth, their nice clothing, and even their food. As I looked up at the ceiling, I could feel my bottom lip quiver because I knew exactly what it felt like to lose such things.

The heavy, dark feeling enveloped me again, and I had to sit up and open my lungs in order to inhale sufficient air as those awful days during eighth grade flashed before me in patches: the ripped wallpaper and dank smell of the only motel that would admit us; Mom's empty, trance-like stare; the weasel-like, suspicious eyes of the motel manager as he repeatedly asked for rent; my classmates' looks of disgust and scorn at my appearance; my own self-disgust when I looked in the flaked mirror of the creaky bathroom and saw the girl whose father had abandoned her.

The memories made me cough and swallow and want to throw up, but instead I sighed deeply and shut the Book of Mormon. What was the point? I could read this book a hundred times and I would never receive a message from that spirit Alex and James and the missionaries talked about. Even if there were a god, he wouldn't be getting in touch with *me*. Why would he? My own father hadn't found me worth sticking around for.

Even though I told myself otherwise, and even though Dr. Griffin had tried to convince me that what my father had done had nothing to do with me, deep within I suspected it *was* because of me our father had left. That he'd stopped loving me because I wasn't his little princess anymore, because my legs had gotten too long and I was no longer small and cute. But deeper still, I feared he had discovered that I just hadn't been worth loving in the first place.

No, even if there were a god, I was sure he wouldn't feel I was worth his time either. He hadn't been there for us during that awful period, had he? No manna had dropped down from heaven to help us. Oh, no. It'd been up to me. And I'd had to lie and deceive and steal just so my family could survive. At one point I'd gone into the local Giant Eagle and walked out with two boxes of granola bars. I'd taken my least favorite kind just to feel better about it, but I'd taken them. It was Uncle Bartho who'd come to our rescue and "saved" us, not God. Only Uncle Bartho wasn't around anymore. If there were a God, why had he taken Uncle Bartho?

I picked up the paisley pillow and held it between my hands, squeezing the sides together. The truth? The truth was I *wanted* to be in that high building with the good clothes and nice furniture and plenty to eat and where I would at least be *perceived* as somebody of stature and worth. I never wanted to find myself down below in the filthy lowlands again. Oh, James was right—I often acted superior. I tried to dress correctly and look my best and I'd done my share of scoffing at those who didn't. But it was never really the scoffing at others part of being in the "high building" that I found appealing. I just wanted to climb as far away as possible from that sleazy motel that had swallowed our lives. That was something James couldn't have known when he'd had me face the mirror. I suspected that even Alex, as well as he knew me, would never fully understand the strong urgency I felt to make sure we always remained well away from where we'd been.

I took another deep breath and blew it out slowly. Maybe I didn't even want there to be a god! If there were a god who knew everything, not only would he know about some of the less-than-saint-like things I'd done in order to survive, but he'd also know the whole ugly truth: Even though I looked good on the outside, inside things weren't lined up correctly and probably never would be again.

Even if Dr. Griffin had been right about my having been perfectly acceptable before my father left, I wasn't acceptable any longer. Perhaps it was true that I could repent of some of the things I'd *done*—the missionaries said we could repent of almost anything—but there was little I could do about what I'd *become* inside. There was something very basic missing inside me and bitterness and anger had filled in the gap.

There was a hatred there as well. Hatred for my father who had left us. In fact, there were days when I hated my father so much that I found myself hoping something terrible had happened to him. Sometimes I was so angry that I would whisper aloud to

Uncle Bartho, or to that god I didn't even believe in, that I hoped my father was dead.

I highly doubted that harboring such feelings would qualify a person like me for "sainthood." A god, in the unlikely case that there was one, would know that inside I didn't come close to being in the emotional and spiritual shape it would take to join a church that required nothing less than full and complete commitment.

Chapter Twenty-Nine

O nly two days after I'd broken the news to my brother and James and the missionaries that this time I was firm in my decision to discontinue my studies of the Mormon faith, James received his mission call from Salt Lake City. It wasn't a phone call at all, as I'd expected, but a large packet of papers in a white envelope.

"You read it, Jana," he said, pulling out the packet and handing it to me. "The rest of us are too nervous!"

"Dear Elder Wickenbee," I somehow managed to pull out of my mouth. "You are hereby called to serve as a missionary of The Church of Jesus Christ of Latter-day Saints in"—I paused and looked up with what I hoped was a smile—"the Philippines Quezon City Mission."

"The Philippines!" Mama Wickenbee, the sought-after chemist, hurried to the desk to get the world globe while Papa Wickenbee, the genius physicist, rushed to pull out volume P of an old *World Book* encyclopedia set. They both came back crying.

"It's so far!" Mary Jane cried. "They're sending my boy so far!"

"I thought Philippines had two L's," moaned Rudolf, his pudgy face bright red. "I don't even know how to spell it, and now my youngest son is going there!" He pulled out a large hanky, wiped his eyes, and blew hard.

I was fully empathizing with Mary Jane and Rudolf and had the urge to cry openly and honk my nose in objection as well. Instead, I bit the inside of my bottom lip hard, which helped me retain my composure.

Just eight weeks later (or two years minus fourteen days ago depending on how—or when—you look at it), I was biting my lip hard again right here at the airport as Alex and I said good-bye to James before his flight to Salt Lake City and the Church's missionary training center. As our dear friend disappeared through the gate, I wondered if I would ever again play chess with him, visit with him, or enjoy his company now that we were literally parting ways.

James's visa was delayed, requiring him to spend some extra time in the MTC. But he hadn't been in the Philipines long when my brother received his own white packet from Utah. I was numb by then.

"Well, at least we know where Montana is and how to spell it," I stated after Michelle had done the honors and had read the first few lines on the top letter. Surprisingly I felt no disappointment whatsoever that Alex was going out west to an area of the country I'd once referred to as a dirt farm and not to a more exotic or culturally significant area of the world. I was actually highly relieved my twin brother was staying stateside, and I studied his face to see how *he* felt about the assignment.

Uncle Phil wondered too. "Are you disappointed you're not going foreign?" he asked Alex gently.

"No, Man, if Montana is where the Lord needs me, then Montana is exactly where I want to be!"

"Good attitude!" Phillip extended his hand to Alex as Ruthie beamed at them both. She hugged her nephew, then slipped him a card with what I assumed contained a check made out for the same generous amount she'd presented to James not that long before.

Aunt Nadine tried to calm Reggie, who was crying. "I want to go to the mountains with Alex," he moaned. "Why is Alex going to the mountains?"

"He's going to Montana, Sweetheart. Maybe we can visit him there." Although Nadine had shown some interest in the Mormon Church in the weeks since her sister's baptism, it was obvious she didn't understand fully what a mission was all about. "You'll still be able to attend college while you're preaching, won't you?" she'd asked Alex at one point.

Mom was fanning herself with a tea towel. "I'm sorry. It's wonderful! I'm sorry!"

Michelle didn't seem to be in her normally upscale emotional condition either and had to breathe deeply several times as she widened her eyes. "Let's call Cassie," she said with a shaky laugh. "Cassie needs to be in on this!"

"Okay." I nodded with empathy. I knew exactly why Michelle

wanted to call Cassie. Maybe Cassie would help *me* feel better as well when she blasted her excitement through the airways. "Put her on speaker," I suggested.

Cassie didn't disappoint us. She not only blasted out her excitement about Alex's missionary call, but then had us all laughing as she told us how she'd hula-ed off another fifteen pounds. Hula was now her exercise of choice and we laughed again thinking she was kidding when she said she wanted to fly to Hawaii and teach it there someday.

Alex wanted to talk to Bud about *his* plans and he turned off the phone speaker. A few seconds later we heard Alex say, "Of course you're not too tall to be a missionary. Missionaries come in all sizes." Then, "Well, I agree with James. You'd be getting noticed for a good cause."

Next we called Sadie, who told us her cousin—and our friend Derrick—had joined the army. "Oh, my gosh," I said, "Derrick in the army?" I'm sorry to admit that it did at that moment occur to me that basic training would reinforce and solidify the habits I'd tried so hard to help Derrick cultivate. I very much doubted a drill sergeant would put up with any chicken pecking, but still, I worried about Derrick's sensitive psyche.

We knew that Terrance had been attending Princeton, where I hoped he was still swinging his arms and keeping his mouth closed. Nobody had heard from Garlia or some of the other former committee members for some time, but Sergei had returned to Moscow.

Sadie was still speaking quietly. "Michelle thinks I should take some college bookkeeping or accounting classes."

"How do you feel about that?"

"I'm not sure. They really rely on me at Barnie's Bowl."

"It never hurts to improve your mind," I said, "and who knows, maybe someday you could become Barnie's head accountant." There was a long snortless pause as if she were digesting that. "Well, give it some thought," I said.

After Alex had called Paul, Terrance, Butch, and several other friends, Phil suggested we all go get ice cream to celebrate. I declined and went straight to my room. I had a political science test the next day. I'd started college the semester before at Cleveland State and tests stop for no man—or woman—not even someone who has a twin brother about to leave her for two long years.

Yes, Cleveland State. Even though I'd been accepted to Harvard and had been thrilled at the prospect, I just couldn't bring myself to turn down a full scholarship here at home. With all his savings and summer earnings going to his mission, Alex would need tuition money when he came back. And even though Mom insisted we were in excellent shape financially and was beside herself with disappointment about my decision, the large chunk from our savings that Harvard and all it represented would deduct had simply made me feel too insecure. I knew how quickly a rug, even an Aubusson, could be pulled out from under a family.

Fortunately, thus far I'd been pleasantly surprised and even impressed with Cleveland State. I discovered within only a week of classes that strong capable women are far better accepted on a college level than they are in junior high and high school. They've appreciated my opinions at Cleveland State and, as usual, I've been happy to share those opinions. Within two weeks, professors were turning to me for answers. That's why I felt such an urgency to prepare and study for my upcoming test even as my family celebrated Alex's missionary call. But I'd only reviewed two paragraphs when it hit me in the pit of my stomach that my twin brother would soon be leaving and for two years I wouldn't have the opportunity to go out for ice cream with him.

I grabbed my keys, rushed out to Uncle Bartho's BMW, and sped to Farr's Better Ice Cream Parlor, where Alex and the rest of our family and friends had headed.

Chapter Thirty

ᐁ

Life is full of ironies. Soon I, a professed agnostic, was writing to two Mormon missionaries. And what a contrast their letters have been! Before his mission president whisked James off to the Quezon City mission headquarters as one of his assistants, my friend worked in a mile square area that housed a million people. He sent a photo of himself in an old World War II jeepney, holding a cage of chickens for a Filipino traveler. "There's too much traffic and congestion for bikes," James explained, "so we rely on public transportation."

Montana, on the other hand, was all about space. The population of Darby where Alex is working right now has nine hundred cows and one hundred people. Alex sent a photo of himself in a cowboy hat and boots holding up a branding iron with the notation: "I think I'm starting to get the language! 'Purteneer' means 'just about.'"

"Speaking 'cowboy' just might get you into politics after all," I wrote back. I knew Alex would know I was joking and that I've fully come to terms with the fact that politics isn't where he wants to be. He's thinking now of eventually moving west to teach science. The main thing is he's happy. And how can I complain, really? I nagged him to go somewhere and be something, didn't I? My brother did exactly that. He went to Montana and became a missionary. I envy the simplicity of his life.

This past year, a couple of James's and Alex's letters have been almost identical. For example, I received a lengthy letter from James concerning repentance and the atonement. Just a short while after that I received a similar letter from Alex. Both urged me to resume studying Mormon doctrine and praying. But I'd moved on.

That spring, after Alex left, I immersed myself in my studies, toes and all. I had a mission of my own—a quest! I wanted to *be* the know-it-all James had accused me of being. My plan was simple. I would learn everything there was to know in every academic area.

When I wasn't working for Adriana's dad in his financial planning firm, I devoured textbooks whole, researched for hours at the library, and wrote endless papers.

I finished off my second semester courses that first year, then plunged into just as difficult a summer schedule. But it didn't take me many weeks into the summer to recognize that what James had told me a couple of years or so before was true: The more I learned, the more I realized there was to learn. I'd had no choice but to come to the conclusion that even if I studied every minute of my entire life, my knowledge would only be a minuscule grain of sand in comparison to all there was to learn.

Even more frustrating was my realization that I couldn't even rely on those theories I'd once considered well-established and irrefutable enough to be factual. One of my professors showed us an article about new findings which indicated modern man did not descend from the Neanderthal after all, but from upright beings who looked as we do now. Then my anthropology professor joked that the questions on his midterms hadn't changed for several years, but the correct answers had. I didn't find his comment humorous. I guess I still longed for something stable and concrete to hold on to—something like that rod I'd read about once.

Still disillusioned with my efforts to know it all or make sense of anything, at the end of the summer I decided to add a new dimension to my life. I acted on my brother's high school suggestion that *I* be the one in the family to enter the political arena. I applied for and was selected to serve as one of the university's eight student body vice presidents.

"I'm helping run this school," I wrote to Alex at the beginning of last semester. "Maybe I'm swimming in a small, less-than-prestigious pond, but I *am* meeting the right people."

"What do you mean—the *right* people?" Alex shot back. "What are the qualifications for being the *right* kind of person?" It was a typical Alex inquiry.

I wadded up his letter. Was he insinuating once again that I couldn't tell true worth? Did he think that I was planning to dump old friends for new ones? Or that I was choosing to associate with only an elect few? Well, he was wrong. I have friends from every walk of life now. As a matter of fact, I've still kept in touch with those friends who helped Alex, James, and I accomplish what we refer to as the Super-Jim/Super-Fairport Miracle. I not only e-mail Cassie frequently, but Michelle and I eat lunch with Sadie every other week.

At our last get-together, I sought their input concerning my aspiration of running for president of Cleveland State at the end of this next year. "You're a future accountant," I'd said to Sadie, whose still longish, but stylish bangs were swept to the side, revealing her nothing-to-be-ashamed-of high cheekbones and small dark eyes. "Do you think I'd get the votes?"

"I think you have a very good chance," she said after a few seconds of careful thought.

Michelle agreed, her lighter, larger eyes reflecting the same sincerity. "Sadie's totally right. You've really made a name for yourself up here. It's amazing how many people seem to know you and respect you. Go for it!" It was exactly what I was hoping to hear.

Michelle had a dental appointment and after she hurried off, Sadie and I visited a little longer and caught up on her cousin and our other old friends. Then Sadie was quiet and I sensed she had something more to say.

"Michelle's been wanting me to take the lessons from the Mormon missionaries," she stated. She studied my face and I could tell she was waiting for me to express my opinion on this news.

"It never hurts to learn new things," I said at once. "And as religions go, I think the Mormon Church is one of the best. Its

precepts make sense and it sets high standards for its members."
Who was I to dissuade Sadie? The Mormon Church could possibly
do more for Sadie than hours with a top therapist. Look what one
of its members had done for the students of a high school by a
lake.

"You took the lessons, didn't you?"

"Yes."

Again, I could tell Sadie wanted more information and I
pushed at the remaining crust of my peach cobbler, then looked
up. "I'm not religious. I'm not even sure that I believe in a god." I
opened my mouth again, but realized even if I'd wanted to,
I couldn't explain something I didn't understand myself. In fact it
was still a sensitive, hurtful area for me, one I tried not to delve
into often.

"Well, I believe in God and I pray every day," Sadie said with
intensity. "I've always believed in a god and his angels. I think God
helped me become friends with you and Michelle." She smiled
then and there was such peace in her button eyes that for a few
moments, I envied Sadie her simple faith.

Now *I* became pensive as I thought about how she'd told me
that Derrick might soon be deployed. "Maybe you should suggest
that the Mormon missionaries contact Derrick too." I was worried
about his sensitive soul and guessed he would need all the spiritual comfort he could get.

"I think that's a very good idea," Sadie said without hesitation.
Then Sadie studied my face carefully for a few seconds. "If you
want to win the election and get more votes, you need to smile

more." She pulled back, a corner of her mouth twitching with surprise at her courage.

I giggled slightly. "Oh! Oh, okay, well thanks for the tip." It was something James had neglected to mention when he'd had me face the mirror and pointed out all my flaws, but I recognized the comment might have some merit. "You may be right," I said.

"I *am* right," said Sadie. "You have nice teeth and you're beautiful and smart. You have everything to smile about." Then she pulled back and grinned. "Maybe you should put masking tape on your wrist so you'll remember."

That made me giggle more and then my giggling inspired Sadie to giggle and soon we seemed to be trying to outdo each other in a snorting contest. She, of course, won. I'm sure the other restaurant patrons wondered about our sanity.

Yes, we'd become pretty good friends, Sadie and I. I was even thinking about talking to Jack, Adriana's dad, about the possibility of hiring Sadie and cutting back my hours.

So how could Alex insinuate I was turning my back on old friends? Still, I asked myself, what could it possibly hurt to also seek out people with clout and connections? My motivations in seeking the presidency of a school were not nearly as pure, altruistic, and unselfish as James's had been, but I had some pretty good ideas and had talked to a lot of individuals about how we could improve Cleveland State. I hoped to guide the students toward a greater desire to serve in the community, the city, and the state, for one thing. In fact, I had some good ideas for society in general if and when I should enter an even bigger political arena.

While Cleveland State wasn't what you could call a prestigious school, it was a start and it was exciting to find myself for the first time in the highest echelons of an organization. Michelle was right. I was well-known and respected and I was socializing with others in the top echelons. I'd even dated a number of top-notch men who had their futures all planned out. There was Julian Gregorson, who planned to attend Duke for his MBA. There was Don Jessop, pre-med, and several others as well.

Soon after I'd replied to my brother's letter, however, Adriana introduced me to someone whose picture I could have sent to my brother with the caption: "The *right* kind of person."

"Miles is pre-law like you and he's planning to go into politics," she'd told me.

"Who isn't?"

"Except this guy has connections. His uncle is Howard Reynolds."

"You mean *the* Howard Reynolds, *Representative* Howard Reynolds, head of the house subcommittee?"

"That's right."

I found myself rubbing my fingers together. "I guess that does give Miles somewhat of a toe in the door, doesn't it?" *A toe?* I remember thinking. *More like an entire leg.*

To my surprise, I soon discovered that for someone born with not only a silver spoon, but a full set of polished silverware in his mouth, Miles was a *nice* individual, decent and ethically intact. In fact, the more time I spent with him, the more impressed I became. Like James, Miles was president of his high school student body. Even better, in my estimation, was the fact that he was planning to run for student president of Ohio State University this next year.

"I'm thinking he won't need a makeover," I joked with Adriana.

"I'm thinking you're right about that," she responded with a chuckle and a double eyebrow lift.

I *was* right. Miles already wore the right clothes; held himself properly; and his teeth were cloud-white. He had even had laser surgery on his eyes so he wouldn't need contacts.

"You don't by any chance play chess, do you?" I asked him not long ago over a pleasant supper of pheasant under glass at the Lakeshore Country Club.

"I do," he said as he patted his mouth with his napkin.

"Why doesn't that surprise me?"

He smiled mysteriously, humbly, yet confidently. "I'm glad we have so much in common," he said as he took my hand, "because I have plans for us." He paused and looked into my eyes with orbs that rivaled James's in blueness. "Let me know when you're ready to hear about them."

Yes, Miles was the walking definition of what I once considered class. He had all the important finishing touches—all "the right stuff."

After he dropped me off that night, I stayed up until early in the morning making an extremely long list of all Miles's "qualifications" and all the advantages of thinking seriously about someone who had hitched his wagon to a star and had, in not so many words, invited me to hitch a ride with him.

It wasn't until about two A.M. that I stopped my frantic listing, sighed, crumpled up the sheet, and threw it across the room because once again it was no use! This session would end just as all the other sessions had ended. As perfect as Miles Reynolds seemed to be and as long as his list of qualifications might become, there was just one little thing wrong with him: He wasn't James.

My correspondence with James has confirmed to me that there is nobody I feel as comfortable, yet intellectually stimulated with. The letters have also reconfirmed that there is nobody funnier, more interesting, kinder, more sensitive, and more morally intact than James Orville Wickenbee, my true friend and confidant.

Adriana thought I was completely out of my mind when I told her about my plans to let Miles know I consider him just a friend.

"Look, I know you've pulled this on other guys and I thought you were crazy then, but Miles Reynolds is not just anyone, Jana. You just don't run into someone like him more than once in a lifetime. And it's obvious he's crazy about you! You'd be an absolute fool to throw this one back. Do you know how many girls—including me—would give their eyeteeth to have him?"

Her hair, which was a little more pink than usual, was sticking up at odd angles and she was wearing her dance clothes with a shawl over them. After I'd talked to her over the phone, she had immediately rushed over to my house to dissuade me in person from following through on what she considered a "ludicrous" plan. Now she was following me around Alex's room as I fed his pets.

"Think about what you'd be throwing away! There's a good chance Miles will be president of Ohio State at the same time you're president of Cleveland State college. How perfect is that? And do you understand what this guy could do for your political career afterwards? Not to mention the amazing personal life you'd have. Do you even have an inkling of how well-heeled and socially registered his family is?"

"I think I do," I said, wincing only a little as I dumped the mealworms into the gecko cage, the most disgusting part of feeding Alex's animals.

After I'd filled the hamsters' little water bin and had begun peeling off the latex gloves, thinking I was finished, I realized Adriana was not finished. She still had one last blow. One that hit me right where it really hurt.

"I seriously hope you're not getting rid of Miles because you think something is going to happen between you and James."

I left the gloves dangling from my fingers for a second or two as I stared at the hamster cage. When I didn't respond, Adriana continued. "Look, Jana, I know—*everybody* knows—that James is a super human being. He proved that in high school and there's no question about that." She was speaking slowly and quietly now. "But, he's a Mormon, remember? If you're dumping Miles because you're thinking there's some future with a Mormon missionary, you need to wake up and smell the coffee, Lady. You do still drink it, right?"

"I do," I said, my throat dry. I finished pulling off the gloves, deposited them in the trash, and lowered myself to the edge of Alex's bed.

Adriana was completely correct. There was no future with James. Yes, it was true Phil had married my Aunt Ruthie before she was officially a member of the Mormon Church, but James had made it clear that it was extremely unusual for a Mormon missionary to come back and marry someone who was not even a member. *Pretty much unheard of.* Those had been the exact words. Oh, yes, I'd thought of those words often. Now I stared at Alex's favorite hamster Kumo, who was ferociously circling his tiny Ferris wheel and I blinked slowly.

"Point made?" asked Adriana.

"Point made," I repeated. I felt like crying.

— ᴏᴆ —

I feel like crying here at the airport as I lay down my magazine and once again press my knuckles together. Now that I've reviewed everything, I'm feeling more confused and hopeless than ever. The fact that Dolly Devonshire, who *did* stop drinking coffee and was baptized last year, has just come out of the elevator isn't helping much.

Dolly's hair is streaked just a little darker and she's looking classier than ever in a blousy shirt and nice-fitting Levis that I would have picked out for myself. Yes, Dolly Devonshire, it turned out, isn't such a goofus. She's been accepted into the nursing program at Ohio State. Arriving with her is Shereen Quinn, who was recently crowned Miss Cleveland on an abstinence until marriage platform.

The girls are creating quite a scene. Butch Torkinson has grabbed Dolly from behind and is swinging her around. My view is blocked by some Asian students with backpacks, seemingly hundreds of them, and when I finally catch sight again of the group waiting for James, I naturally assume that it's Butch who has lifted Dolly to his shoulders where James will see her first thing.

Only then I realize that it's Terrance. I'm pleased that someone from our old committee group who I'd hoped would be here actually *is* here. Yes, it's normally shy Terrance, all right, who has lifted Dolly high into the air. How did she get him to do that? But why am I surprised? Dolly has that effect on people. According to Cassie, Dolly helped inspire Bud to finally send in his mission papers with just three exuberant words: "You should go!"

Why doesn't Dolly find her own friends? I wondered then and I'm wondering now. In fact, I sit back down, blink slowly, and chew on my perfectly polished nails.

When I look back up at the monitor, I see that Northwest Flight 107 has arrived.

Chapter Thirty-One

A s passengers stream through the main airport corridor, I look around to make sure I'm clear, then stand and strain to see in the direction of the security gate. Rudolf is doing his best to hold Mary Jane back, possibly realizing that if she breaks through security, they'll need to shut down the airport. She's a mess. If my mother hadn't been in charge of still another Relief Society service project, she would have been here to help Rudolf and James's brother Felix restrain Mary Jane and keep her under control.

I put on my glasses, then lower myself to my seat, and take them off. I stand again. *Is he here?* I step forward, move back again, advance several more steps, edging around a man in a kilt who's struggling with a bagpipe. Again I hesitate.

Terrance has lowered his shoulder so that Dolly can jump down, and now she's moving forward with Shereen right on her heels. Others move forward as well. In fact I think for a moment that I see Garlia, but of course it isn't Garlia. I wish it were, but she's in rehab just like Lyla Fannen was at one time. Drugs apparently cross class barriers. No, it's someone else who's come with Terrance. A girlfriend!

Okay, okay, this is it. I pull back my shoulders and lift my head as if strings are pulling me up. *Smile,* I think, and I do because I've been following Sadie's advice. In fact, I smile as if I have all the confidence in the world. *Act as if . . . Act as if . . .*

I can handle this. Dolly, Shereen? I can handle them. But I've only taken five or six additional steps in the direction of the group when an unusual yet somewhat familiar shade of red catches my attention. It's a subtle fox-red, a one-of-a-kind color.

The man with the bagpipe has moved forward along with me and has somehow maneuvered his way in front of me and is blocking my view again. I move around his bagpipe, slip my glasses back on and strain to see past him. I've met only one person with hair that exact color. When I'm finally able to see in that direction again, I catch my breath.

Lyla Fannen, our formidable high school enemy, is standing pensively at an adjacent window. Looking as amazingly beautiful as ever, she takes an uncertain step or two forward toward the group, then a step back.

My mouth has fallen open. I'm barely breathing as I realize that the girl who abused and harassed us in high school, the girl who caused James to fall on his face on stage in front of the entire high school student body, the girl whose aim in life was to destroy us, has had the audacity to come to the airport and is standing just a hundred feet away from me. But why?

Of course I've heard the rumors that after hitting rock bottom, going through three rehab programs, she's finally recovered and is back in the area, but what possible reason would she have for being here at the airport? I shake my head. *My stars, don't tell me she considers herself one of James's friends!*

I pull back around the man with the bagpipe, who seems determined to always be in my way, and slit my eyes to look for Lyla's telltale lifted eyebrow, but I don't see it. Lyla's body language seems to be indicating a lack, rather than an overabundance, of pride. The chin is lowered, not lifted.

What is going on? I wonder to myself. Has the horrible but exquisite Lyla Fannen suddenly done one of those all too common inner overhauls? A magical flip through some revolving door? Has she too had some kind of a spiritual rebirth? Well, that's convenient, isn't it? I shudder at the implications.

Yes, it could be that Lyla somehow ended up on the list of people that Mary Jane sent James's letters to monthly. It could also be that James has been writing personal notes of inspiration to this witch disguised as a beauty. He *did* feel sorry for her when he heard about her problems. Has he somehow, in some fashion, helped her get to this point?

My stomach is churning and my throat is so tight I can barely get air. So Lyla has popped back alive and well and has returned from the dead to be right here at the airport. Well, this is too much! I can handle the Backus sisters being here and even Dolly and Shereen but *this?* No, not this! As I begin to move sideways I bump into a woman hauling a huge drawstring bag over her shoulders. "Are you here for James too?" I feel like asking her.

My heavens, why on earth did I come? Why have I been sitting here this entire evening waiting for James when it's completely obvious he doesn't need me here. He has a half-dozen newly reformed young women here. He even has the new and improved Lyla Fannen here, of all people. Well that's fine, just fine, because I don't even want to see him!

Freeing myself of the bagpipe man and a lady dragging some kind of beanbag chair, I move sideways and begin sprinting down the long corridor. I'm an idiot! I should never have dumped Miles Reynolds.

Anger has taken over the pain now and I throw the magazine on a nearby chair, loop my bag over my shoulder, and begin swinging my arms like a windmill as I hurry away faster and faster. Why would I even want to see James? *He's nothing but a . . .* I shut my eyes and begin to slow down. What was I about to say? Was I really about to call James a *Flashy Floyd?* Was I really putting him in the same league as the scoundrel playboy ex-husband who nearly killed off Auntie Ruthie?

I reach for the nearest chair and sit down and blow out air. Trying to make James appear less than he is, placing blame on him just because I can't have him is completely lying to myself. As much as I'd like to be able to accuse James of being a vile, deceitful villain right now, the truth is just the opposite and I know it and if I believed in a god, he'd know it too. No, I can't lie to myself. I need to accept facts.

The truth is, I know James thoroughly and have for quite a while. There's absolutely nobody less deceitful and more humble and genuine and kind. I may be angry and disappointed, but I can't deny that. I sniff and push out a laugh of self-disgust as

I admit that any expectations were of my own making, my own imaginings. James never once made any promises to me. He owes me nothing. If all kinds of people—even supposedly repentant villainesses like Lyla—are drawn to him, it's just because . . . well, that was established a few years ago in a high school he helped make over. James is a spiritual makeover artist who draws out the good—the very best—in people.

Yes, well, I get up and start moving again. The truth of the matter is he's too good for me—that's the whole problem here. James is pure and guileless and selfless and he's, well, filled with light. Oh, he tried to help me. So did Alex. But you can only work with those basics you have to work with. Yes, I may look good and maybe my chin is no longer lifted and I've softened on the surface and improved my personality and definitely my people skills, and okay, I guess I'm even a little kinder, but when you delve deeper, I'm still that same shabby, fearful, resentful, ugly mess of a girl that I can't seem to get away from.

I pick up my pace and I'm passing the Hertz rental booth when I hear my name.

Across the wide corridor, Michelle and Sadie are slowing down to meet me. Sadie is lifting her hand with concern.

"Where are you going?" Michelle calls out.

I shake my head at my friends and motion for them to move forward and join the rest of the adoring fans waiting to see James. "Go ahead," I call.

Yes, go join Ruby and Topaz and Dolly and Shereen! Go join Lyla Fannen! "Go see Mr. Power," I mutter to myself as I feel their eyes following me. I sense that Sadie is thinking about coming after me and I turn. Sure enough she is taking some steps in my direction.

"Go on," I motion her away. I turn and hurry away even faster so she'll recognize that it's futile to try to catch up.

Life really is ironic, I'm thinking a moment or two later as I come to the end of the terminal. *Strange.* Because as things turned out, the James I thought I transformed into a superhero always was a superhero and always did possess a strength and power of a far different nature than I once thought was important. Power that . . .

It isn't James's power. The phrase hits me with force and I pull to a stop, confused. The words aren't audible, at least not to my ears, but I *feel* them clearly. In fact, I'm still feeling them. They're penetrating my entire being to the extent that I find myself limping to the nearest chair.

The feeling isn't entirely foreign. It's similar to feelings I used to brush off as emotional reactions. It's similar to feelings I've felt at those instances when I did something right or good or kind, or when my heart was touched. In fact I felt something like it just yesterday when I talked to Jack about hiring Sadie. Only this time the feeling is stronger and deeper.

It isn't James's power. Then whose power is it? I don't need to ask.

But this can't be happening! I don't want it to be happening. There are ramifications. I went over this a long time ago and determined then that my ineligibility for religion runs deep for reasons I just reviewed. No. I take a deep breath. I'll be okay because this isn't real. I've taken philosophy and biology and this goes counter to everything I've learned in these classes. It simply isn't happening. It absolutely can't be happening. And yet I know it happened.

It is *still* happening whether I want to believe in this or not. But why?

If this is honestly that Holy Spirit that the missionaries and James and Alex and others have told me about, then what would be the point? Where could it possibly lead? What good would it do? If there were a god, he'd know that trying to change me is useless. I'm ugly inside. I lift my face to the ceiling wondering if I might actually see something up there, but I see only a ceiling. I lower my eyes, blinking frantically.

For the first time I notice where I am. I'm sitting straight across from a baggage check-in desk where people of all kinds are checking in their luggage for their upcoming flights. A heavyset brown man who looks like a darker version of Uncle Bartho is turning his suitcases over to the smiling attendant. Next in line is a young mother, struggling not only with her bags, but two toddlers. Are they twins? In the next check-in spot, an employee lifts the bags of a well-dressed and sophisticated looking woman with an obvious attitude. The nerds, the geeks, the suave, the sleek—all types are waiting to check in their bags.

A sound, something partway between a laugh and a cry escapes from my lips and I try to choke it back as I realize that what I'm seeing before me is symbolic of what Alex and James have been trying to tell me about repentance and the atonement.

James told me that it's not just our sins Christ takes upon him but all our negative feelings, all our disappointments and pain, all the bad things that have ever happened to us, all our burdens, and yes, all our baggage. His words hadn't registered before, but they do now as I realize that if it's all true, then I wouldn't need to do it alone—none of us would.

I sit up a little straighter as everything I learned from the missionaries, everything I did not accept because I did not think I was acceptable, floods back to me: Jesus, our brother, gave his life for us, and God, our literal father, allowed him to do it for *us*. Could it really be true? It can't be! There are too many unanswered questions! I still don't understand how it all fits together and works! And yet the warmth has filled me to capacity. The comforting feeling is soothing me and encouraging me and bringing with it *hope.*

When I look back at the line of people I notice that an older woman has stepped in to help the young mother tend her twins. A few yards back in line, a father is reaching down to help his little boy heft a suitcase too heavy for him to lift alone. The magnificence of what I'm seeing engulfs me.

If we're really all God's children, it means we're all siblings. Just as Alex and I once shared a womb, we all once lived together with Him. I realize that if this is true, life is not a game of chess or an election with winners and losers. There is no need to step on one another to get where we think we want to be because we're not here to compete. No, if God is our literal father then we're all in this life together and another's successes are our own. It's about love.

James, I realize, had been smart enough to tap into the power that we all have access to. For the first time I understand his approach to life. *God is good,* I remember hearing at my Great-Aunt Beatrice's Protestant meetings when I was little. *God is love.* And now something even more odd is happening. I'm feeling it myself—love.

Just that simply, I've released any negative feelings I've ever felt toward anyone. I'm feeling love toward everyone here at the airport. In fact, I'm feeling warmth and love and goodwill toward everyone in the entire world, in the whole universe, in all universes. I'm even feeling goodwill toward Dolly Devonshire and Lyla Fannen. Yes, Lyla Fannen!

I laugh aloud, this time sincerely and with joy. It no longer bothers me that she's here or that any of them are here. Because, oh beautiful stars, I honestly think I want the best for them—for all of them, even Lyla. But then I pull in my breath.

What about my father who abandoned Alex and me when we needed him most—who left us and Mom to struggle on our own until we ended up in those nasty circumstances? What about him? Can I honestly forgive him?

It comes to me that if I have a Heavenly Father who is always there and will never leave me then I don't need to keep harboring the anger I've felt all these years toward my very human dad. I can love even him. I huff out a sob as I recognize that a part of me always did.

I'm so filled with good, positive, and warm feelings now that it's as though I've gone through some kind of spiritual revolving door and am swooping through the skies above the airport, above the houses and the tall buildings, above everything that's of this world. I am realizing that if we're all children of God then I am a child of God too!

Okay, okay, I try to get my bearings. Am I losing my mind?

What's happening here? Is this some kind of a convenient psychological phenomenon? Cynicism and doubt again seep in. Of course it is. That's got to be it. These kinds of things don't happen! They don't! Not to me. There are still all those unanswered questions and none of this makes sense.

But deep in my soul it feels real and I'm rising again back into the sky and I'm soaring again. In fact, I'm filling up with urgency as well. If there's even a remote possibility that these feelings really are from God and that I am his child and that he really cares enough about me that he just sent me a message, then I've got things to do! I need to start reading and studying again. I need to start attending church. I need to start praying like crazy, only deeply and sincerely this time, and doing my utmost to connect. I take a deep breath. I need to write Alex and get his take on this. Should I share this with Mom? I think I will.

And James! My dear friend James will explain to me what just happened. James! I jump up with amazing energy and twirl in the direction of the security gate. James is *here!* He's right here at the airport!

I take off running. One of my sandals slips off and I stop, hop back to get it, and with it still half flopping, I continue. As I get closer, I can see and hear the greetings, yelps of joy, and the commotion. I grab the loose sandal, leap on a chair, and rise to my toes, pressing my hand to my cheek. Yes, he's here!

I see Mary Jane hanging onto his arm, and his dad has him around the waist. They're blurry, but I recognize Phillip and Ruthie. There's James's brother Felix talking to Sadie. There's

Terrance with that someone who looks a little like Garlia. There's Butch. James is greeting all of them, including each anxious girl.

Where are my glasses? Didn't I throw them in my shoulder bag when I started to hightail it? I can't find them. As I push my hand into the side pocket of my bag, I touch the frames and pull them out. I put them on for the umpteenth time in the last hour, only this time I'll leave them on. I want to see James clearly, and I don't care if I look bad in them. I don't care if everyone here thinks I look ghastly. Amazingly, it doesn't matter to me anymore.

I push the glasses higher up on my nose. I laugh aloud because I can see James clearly now and he's wearing glasses too. They're not his new ones—those had been so flimsy they probably only lasted a few weeks in the mission field. No, these glasses are even funnier-looking than the glasses I convinced him to replace all those years ago. They're monstrous, hideous glasses. They're outrageous! James looks like a complete geekkenstein in those glasses—much worse than before. But it doesn't matter because he's still James.

I laugh again because he's peering over these glasses now, scowling and leaning forward far too much. I stop laughing and a little thrill runs through me as he keeps looking around.

Is he looking for me? He is! My eyes well up and I jump down from the seat and find myself running toward James and toward the rest as well—toward all of them!

"Wowsers!" I hear myself shouting. "Double . . . no triple . . . no *quadruple* Wowsers!"

About the Author

Born in the Netherlands, Anya Bateman came to Salt Lake City as a child and discovered early how much she enjoyed language, words, and writing. She attended both Brigham Young University and the University of Utah, graduating from the latter with an English degree and a creative writing emphasis.

Anya's stories and articles have appeared in the Church magazines as well as national magazines such as *Reader's Digest.* She is the author of three books: *Corker, Big Ben Is Back,* and *I Didn't Place in the Talent Race, but . . .*

Anya served a mission to California and has served in several auxiliary leadership positions in the Church. She and her husband are the parents of four children and the grandparents of six.